no

no

Clarence Major

Emerson Hall Publishers, Inc.
New York

3/1973
Gent

ISBN: 0–87829–006–0
Library of Congress catalog card number: 72–92134

FIRST EDITION

Manufactured in the United States of America

contents

1

influence
of
the
moon

Very early in this life I was forced into a silly marriage, but fortunately it was just a church game my enforcers were playing. It wasn't until years later, when my wife, Oni Dunn, and I became sad lovers that I began to truly discover myself. No; maybe it, the discovery, started before that. Maybe it dates back before the time Moses shot Veronica, Gal, Twinkie, me, and himself. Certainly the trauma of it is still with me. And the death of the old man, Grady. Those flies that crawled over his face. The long unconscious and physical torture at the mercy of Slick and Thursday and others. But when Oni and I left the country together, that in itself certainly was a step. Yes. The beginning of a larger self-awareness and liberation; the crisis of such a transformation, led me, I now suspect, into that terrible bullring during a dangerous bullfight in a strange country. And even that, as foolish as it seems, symbolized a very necessary stance because somehow it gave me a sudden vision of how *naked* my presence in the world really is. How absolutely unsafe I'll always be. Anyway, if my luck is as good as your own you'll get your curious eye filled with your end of the bargain. This is news that you can see, possibly live with, certainly survive. I didn't realize that I was really trying to crash out of a sort of penal system in which I was born and grew up. Looking back though, I do realize that the activity of my life indicates merely the position of various political, social, and moral incidents.

It wasn't really a prison except in an abstract social sense and also in a very personal sense. In truth no one ever really could point out where it began or ended, and it wasn't limited to one country. When Oni and I went away together to Latin

America, we were still in it. That's how elusive it was; and it was always shifting. It had so many levels and there were so many ways you could define it. Many people never even once thought of it as an actual prison.

Inside and very close to the beginning, when Moses and Veronica were sort of in control of our area, I remember how things began to fall apart. Things always fall apart but I don't always remember how it happens.

It just so happens that no one, in those days, knew that I was an inspector. Not that being an inspector was ever really *so much,* but it was better than being a guard, like Moses. But that's just my opinion. Anyhow, Moses and Veronica and everybody else thought of me as, and called me, the Boy. I was, to hear them tell it, their offspring, and my name, as I say, was sometimes, Moses Westby.

I had a special thing for lights and clarity and one of the first promises I made to myself was, if I ever got enough authority inside the penal system, I would immediately look into this morbid habit the institution had of never even trying to achieve its stated objective, that is, to rehabilitate us.

But the business about lights is something I'll have to go into separately because most people don't understand what I'm talking about when I'm on the subject. A light, you see, was my very *first* experience.

It was an unused lamp that could never be reached because it stood so high on a portable clothes closet like the sun stands high on a mountain. Sometimes.

The four of us lived in a house where the bleak walls defined for us the poverty and the shape of our dark souls. And that lamp that might have burned was never lit. But it would be untrue to say that I wanted to climb up, take it down, and light it. No; what I really wanted was to break it, like I broke and wrecked other things, to get a sense of my own power.

Moses was in solitary confinement and Veronica was in bed at home in prison and me and Gal were on either side of her, close. She smelled of Vicks Vapor Rub and the edges of her white nose were red; the rims of her eyes were hot metal. The tip of Gal's chocolate face bobbed on the other side. Her toes

4

were wiggling and for all I know she may have been trying out a new dance—

If you go away, Veronica, I said, will we die?

She couldn't nor did she try to answer me. She looked down at me for awhile then turned away, tears brimming her eyes. Suddenly her chest heaved and she started sobbing beyond control. And it was contagious.

Do you understand *why* Moses isn't here with us? Veronica plied, searching leisurely our faces.

I tried to be very hip about it. He's in solitary confinement. I thought, in saying that, I'd demonstrated googobs of wisdom!

Gal quickly added, *And* he's restricted to bread *and* water. Right, Veronica?

Yes, said Veronica. *His sin, is the crime* known as *being himself.*

Silence fell; and Gal and I waited for Veronica to go on. I watched her dabble her knuckles at her wet eyelids.

I don't expect you two to *grasp* all of this, she said; but Moses has never been on good terms with the rulers of this place. I've lived constantly in fear that he'll end on Death Row and in the electric chair, juiced.

A moment later Veronica squeezed us close to her body. And, she closed her eyes as though it were a strain.

At the beginning or end (depending on where *you* begin) of our dull row of cheap dwelling places in a weird vine-covered house lived an angel's bride. She was a feminine demonologist who had a disconcerting habit of tossing her own stale piss out the window of her house that overlooked the public path to the main street. You either had to take this path or the one at the other end and this was the best because it was the easiest. It was no accident that the contents of her slopjar ended all over and dripping off the skin and clothes of men and never women or children. The witch seemed to dislike everybody except young and pretty girls—Veronica, especially, who was twenty years old and quite pretty.

And it was in connection with Veronica (or, as Veronica herself puts it, the Woman) that the old enchanter proved to be one of

5

the few inmates to assert herself forcefully. It was during a morning of fury and horror, while it was raining and thundering. A lot of people were running around fearful of a possible robust full-speed hurricane. The sky had turned black. Dogs were scurrying beneath houses. Twinkie, across the street on her front porch, was singing a song about Hants at Dusk. And it was Dawn. Mr. Hain Alcock, the barber, was running toward his house, his smock flapping wildly about his legs.

Veronica, in her house, was screaming bloody murder. And rightly so. Moses Westby was punching her and kicking her without mercy. He wanted to kill her, he loved her so much. It was the only logical thing he felt he could do to her.

The angel's bride, who sometimes received mail under the strange name, Verdelet, came flying out of her house, galloped across the gravel, shot up the stoop and into Moses' home. The Boy, who was fretting near the door, saw rigid Presbyterian devils leaping naked to a war dance in her eyes. Strapped around Verdelet's waist was a portable whatnot, a kinda cross between a camera and a tape recorder. The old holy virgin snatched the first thing-weapon she saw, which was a broom.

The Boy, meanwhile, rushed the Man and started pounding his tiny fists against the Man's legs. The Man's fist slammed into the Woman's face and the sound of bone breaking filled the house. Irritated by the Boy, the Man turned, and brutally drove a bloody fist between his eyes. The blow landed the Boy on the floor, just as the witch sent sailing her wicked broom handle's tip into Moses' bloodshot right eye.

AAAAAAAAAAAAAAAAH! said Moses. Understandably. He closed his other eye and, with both hands, held the damaged one with loving care.

Let that be a lesson to you, said the sorceress. These were the first *wicce* words anybody'd heard her speak. Her voice was high as the Babia Gora (The Old Woman's Mountain) in Carpathia.

Veronica was in a pool of rich dark blood, sobbing in shock. Gal, the Girl, had screamed and cried herself to sleep, and now sucked loudly on three of her chubby fingers. The Boy got up and stood beside the witch, who stank. He looked at the long black dress with white flowers she wore, then he looked up at

6

her face. She was a gray-looking creature; her face was sunken, tight, mean and though it was wretched it was also somehow sweet and whispered proudly of virginity, even more than membership in the Witches' Sabbath or a summerhome in the spooky terrains of Thuringia.

Moses was out of commission now and he stumbled blindly around grumbling and swearing while Verdelet, on knees and elbows, tried to comfort the Woman on the floor.

You should be fed raw into a meat grinder, the angel's bride said to Moses, who was headed for the back door, where neighbors had gathered. One female neighbor, framed by the window, having seen all the action, called out to the witch: You want I should go get the police?

The witch didn't answer. She was ripping away part of her dress and used the cloth now to dab at the blood pouring from the Woman's face. The woman in the window repeated her question and some one said, *Booooo!* and the angel's bride turned to the faces at the window and spoke. Won't you freaks of artificial insemination ever learn *who* your enemy is? How about one of you husky dittybops coming in here? I need a hand to lift her to the bed.

Meekly, T-Bone, Twinkie's nightrider, entered through the front door, and gave the old woman a hand. After they put the unconscious Woman on the bed, with a pan of warm water and a clean towel, while the Boy stood at her elbow, Verdelet cleaned the matted blood from the Woman's face.

Suddenly, in an insecure tone, the Boy said, She's my delivery woman. And he seemed to have a momentary spasm.

Later that night Moses Westby returned to his home. Veronica was sleeping peacefully, considering the pain she'd endured. Gal and the Boy slept one on each side of her. They were not asleep in his bed. Moses felt a little offended that Veronica was not in his bed where she usually slept. Though he was very drunk he still felt the sharp pain throbbing in his right eye. He looked at the Boy close to the Woman and for a moment felt tempted to kill the Boy. He shuddered and pushed the idea back into some hovel of his mind. What a horrid thought!

7

But then, had he not earlier tried to kill Veronica? He didn't want to think about it, now. Even if "love" had been his impetus, it was better now to think of . . . of what? Of social security, of foreign aid, of that strange gadget the angel's bride wore—what was its function? Moses Westby sat down on the edge of the bed. Gal twitched in her sleep.

The Boy opened one eye.

> *I* opened one eye and looked secretly at Moses. I had loved him and tried to find him many times, but his mentality always escaped, king size, as abstract as the National Debt. Now, he seemed childlike. He looked at Veronica and his mouth fell open to speak.

Veronica, he said, I want to join the NAACP, rewrite all the road signs in the state of Nebraska, join the March on Washington, and learn how to churn butter early in the morning.

I felt Veronica breathing and kinda half expected her to answer. But the silence ticked a second longer.

> Moses Westby scratched his head and murmured, I want a medal for dishonor. Veronica, what I really want is the skill to make paper boats that'll sail across a puddle without getting soggy. Ya know?

Suddenly an immigrant kid from the lowlands of Buttermilk Bottom screams a name.

JUNEBUG!

It made me forget I was holding something inside. And hot stew suddenly weights heavy in the seat of my pants. Now, in great desperation I begin wobbling, not toward the caller, but toward the round stool with the open bottom. And it's too late, obviously. But nevertheless I go through the alley toward the back door, trying to avoid the abuse of the kids but especially Veronica, the Woman. But already laughing kids are following me and the Woman I know will be waiting inside with a belt.

WOOOOOOOOO-WEEEEEEEEEE, cried the children. One of them sticks his head inside the homemade shadows. And shouts unclearly the message of the Boy's deed.

Frantic patterns like you see on a test screen where shots of wave motion of signals carrying fatal information radio warnings of doomsday.

Soon, the Woman *had* to know.

Already the Boy felt the belt against his naked ass. And he knew his playmates wanted to see him get his butt beat blue. They knew the Woman could work at The Boy's punishment with the devotion and skill of a metallurgist doing x-rays of ore.

The Woman smelled him first then came with the belt. The children crowded the backporch, watching her, the belt, and the Boy. They made bets. The Woman was clad in a simple yellow and green housedress. Her hair up in babydoll curls. She was a lovely, emissive beauty. She stood, hands on hips, sadly shaking her head. The stuff had run down into the Boy's

9

shoes, as he tried to climb up onto the stool. He was a mess. Yes, *in* deed.

I got to go to the toilet, he said. I bet you have, she said. She was still shaking her head and also holding her breath, possibly trying not to get too mad. The Girl was taking a nap and the catcalls and hoots and cry for blood from the neighborhood kids were already a bit much. But when the Boy's ass would begin to burn from the stinging caused by the belt the Girl would surely wake from his crying and the Girl would become as per usual a pain-in-the-ass. Though always less so than the Boy.

Even before the Boy knew how to watch people he watched the Woman's face for clues. He listened to her humming, while she scrubbed the crevices of his flesh.

Her singing, when she sang, often concealed the underglow of a secret and quiet building of a plot that brought blisters to rest deep in his flesh. Now, her humming graduated to singing.

And the Boy was fretful despite the obvious *clearing* in the Woman's face. It was a clearing for sympathy but he no longer trusted his own capacity to understand anything. He was being brainwashed? Bit by bit. Learning not to trust his natural intelligence.

The Woman was careful not to get the stuff on her own fingers as she undressed the Boy. *Shit,* she would always say when she got it on her hands. She operated on him very carefully, at arms' length.

And her song was absolutely beautiful.

He was watching the steaming hot soggy red towel she had draped from the edge of the yellow kitchen table.

He stood naked and now damp before her as she with her loafer toe pushed the bundle of his clothing and shoes into a corner. She dreaded the prospect of washing the garments. And she was not reckless enough to throw away the shit.

The kids were crowding the kitchen window now and giggling. Their dark eyes, like reflector bulbs; their bright white teeth clicking above and below their pink tongues. Their elbows bumped and they strained their necks, pushing against one another. If there was profit here, they meant to get it.

10

The Woman applied the hot towel to the Boy's buttocks and listened to him whimper and ask, Are you going to whip me? And she simply continued to sing sweetly while stroking him gently.

But time has a natural way of supplying answers to developmental incidents. No magic, no scholarship, no astrology, no *nothing* really works when it comes to the nature of the future. The moment itself *is* the terror.

With large strokes of scarey love, almost with mechanical solitude, the Woman applied now the belt to the young flesh. With this extension of herself she began to bite deeper and deeper into the spongy dampness of his copper-colored rear end as he screamed *blood*.

And over and over she made him say he would promise to come inside in time to prevent it happening again. And he yelled his promise to the top of his lungs.

And while the kids at the window shouted their joy the Boy discovered in his own moment of frenzy a portion of the clue. It resided in the ritualistic act of being able to give back to the Woman the refrain of her own song. Grasping the clue was one thing, but making it functional was another. The Boy only vaguely understood how the promise of liberation of his spirit could be tapped. And Veronica's song was his only lead.

The Boy and the Girl were peeping.

Twinkie. Funny red-tan face, skinny gal. Dress crammed around her hips, her wet anxious torso groaning beneath the dark figure of her mysterious night-prowling boyfriend. The boyfriend was planted in Twinkie. As they wiggled. And the Boy and the Girl giggled. And Twinkie jumped, throwing the boyfriend off. Twinkie jumps to her flat feet and comes toward us. Her command is harsh: You two *get* in bed!

I'm going to tell Veronica!

Me too, I said.

I'll give you all the ice cream you can eat, tomorrow, if you promise you won't.

We got under the sheet.

She sat down on the side of the bed.

Gal said, Don't want any ice cream. *You were doing it!*

I said, Your boyfriend had his tail in you and you wouldn't let me put mine in you . . .

I will, though, said Twinkie, if you promise not to say anything to Veronica. And *make* Gal promise, too!

Okay, I said, but let me *do it* now.

When my boyfriend leaves. Okay?

Gal sounded like a first-class bitch. She spoke. But I'm gonna tell *anyway!*

Twinkie was desperate. Her gig meant a lot to her. She said, Gal, I'll give you *three* nickels!

Give 'em here.

Twinkie sighed. You have to wait. Can't you wait . . . ?

That's okay, Gal said, I think I'd *rather* tell. I wanna see Veronica clobber the shit outta you.

You're just a tattletale, I said.

Yeah, said Twinkie. And she's a scumbag, too!

I added, just to be mean, And you're a fucking coupon-clipper, too!

Okay, said Twinkie, don't get started bickering, cause you'll be fighting soon. Gal, you aren't really going to say anything about my boyfriend being here, are you?

Yes, I am, and not just to Veronica. I'm planning to tell the guard.

Moses?

Yes, and he'll get the warden to send you to Death Row.

I laughed. Girls never go to Death Row.

They do, *too!* insisted Gal, sitting up furiously against the headboard. Moses told me Cleopatra was juiced with an A & C Grenadier cigar in her mouth, and didn't bat an eyelid.

Gal, said Twinkie, more relaxed now, you're really a sweet person when you want to be, ya know. Isn't she, Moses?

His name isn't Moses! snapped Gal. He's a ladykiller and sometimes our guard calls him C.C. Rider. But the name I like best *on* him is Nicodemus. Gal giggled and covered her mouth.

From the other room we heard Twinkie's boyfriend call, *Twinkie!* And Twinkie said, That's T-Bone. He needs me. I got to go now. (She looked for a moment quite desperate). *Promise me*, she said, looking from Gal's face to mine.

Softly I spoke. I ain't gonna promise you shit. Just get rid of him, send him to the firing squad and come back to me. Come back to Nicodemus, baby!

On hands and knees I crawled to her and mounted her. Her eyes were huge: so close, they frightened me. She was a monster! My fists left their prints in her stomach. Her mouth, to my

13

tongue, was wet and hot and intense. Like the insides of a freshly killed chicken. I expected her to slap me any minute because I was playing around. I knew *how* impatient she could be.

Take off your fucking pajamas, shit!

I began untying them.

Oh, forget it! Leave em on!

I took them off anyway and touched my penis. I watched for her reaction but she gave none.

Meanwhile, Gal, was stone asleep.

The game inventor was looking disdainfully at my organ. Just lie on me, she said, and hold it between my legs; that's *all* you do.

But don't I put it in your peepee hole?

Not if you don't want to get the shit slapped out of you. No, she continued, people don't *ever* do that! Just do as I tell you; and rub it against me. That's all people ever do. They *rub* each other.

Gal, behind us, at the other end of the bed, had suddenly come alive. She spoke harshly: That's not all daddies do to mommies. That's not *how* they make babies!

I was trying to force it in but it was too small and too soft and too short and it kept sliding around and missing the hole. Roughly Twinkie snatched my shoulders and held me firmly against her stomach. With my toes I could touch her knees. My face lay against her breasts.

WILLYA PLEASE CUT THAT SHIT OUT, Twinkie cried in my ear.

Her yelling caused me to cry. And my tears annoyed her even more than my clumsy fingers, my hard-nosed penis.

Stop crying. Come on and do it right. Just move your hips. Don't be wiggling your toes and doing other stupid shit.

I started. Like this?

Yeah; *and hurry and finish!*

14

But you and your boyfriend didn't hurry.

You don't even know how to tell time, Moses, said Gal.

Miss smartass, I said.

I'm gonna tell Veronica.

Well, you won't get any money from me, said Twinkie.

I tried to adjust my prick but the game inventor said: Just leave it alone. Just one more fucking minute and you're getting off me, boy! Anyway, why don't you do it to Gal? She's more your size.

Fuck size.

And *I* don't want *him* to do it to me, anyway.

How come?

Because. Just because.

At some point, the three of us went to sleep. When Veronica returned from where she had been Twinkie went away.

Gal was still asleep while I lay awake watching the delivery woman undress, getting ready for bed. She had taken off everything except her flat black hat with the red flower, her stockings and heels. And she stood now, with a puzzled expression, holding her glossy black purse over her right arm. With her free hand she touched her pop pompadour hairdo. She sat down suddenly on a low stool near the doorway to her bedroom.

I jumped out of bed and went to her. A droplet of snot hung helplessly from her long white nose. But her eyes were blank though wet. I stood before her, wanting to touch her.

She took my hands. Come here, Moses. She pulled me between her thighs and I stood watching her eyes and her mouth.

Why aren't you asleep? she asked.

Because I *hate* you! I snapped.

And she hugged me close. *Yes,* I understand.

Uta was one of my neighbors. Her legs are useless.

Uta speaks: Here.

She hands me the crutches.

Take them.

But how will you stand without them?

Just take 'em.

I put them under each of my arms. I see a giant bug down in a gold-lighted tunnel, carrying a lantern. He's trying to see into the dark pockets, see the gold skulls, the rusty relics of another world. Right under the bed where it's dark. I'm off duty. We're under the delivery woman's and the guard's bed. Uta and I started off playing "house." She was the mother because she didn't want to be the nurse. I was the "father" but I didn't dig it.

Uta's fat soft fingers jump for the wooden footboard of the bed. Otherwise, her sensitive ass would have played pattycake-pattycake-bakers-man with the floorboards. I always think she's gonna hurt herself. Struggling around, the awkward movements. How she manages to take my dick outta my pants even if we're crammed together on the floor in the back of the guard's car. Once in the trunk of another car. And we almost read about ourselves smothered to death in the newspapers.   So, now we're gonna try it under the bed. Though she's a nurse, though I'm an inspector, we don't have as much authority as, say, the tax collector or the guards. Me and the nurse were once caught doing it I don't remember *who* caught us but I dreamed about

it a lot afterwards. The face of the catcher is always blank. Can't see whether it's male or female. But we weren't punished and that was strange because in those days we were not supposed to indulge in sex. It was a luxury for the authorities.
Uta had a fat hairless pink cunt and she believed in lycanthropy. That was all right; I, too, believed in the possibility that human beings could be transformed into animals: we had ourselves as examples.

The crutches, I said.

Pull them under the bed in case somebody comes.

I pull the crutches under to safety. Uta's busy taking out my peter. Her magnetic healing hands. Her sympathetic white magic. She's as white as the delivery woman. Uta strokes it, sings to it. The sweaty odor of her damp forest pumps into my nose. I reach for my mouth but feel my eyes and Uta brings the weight of her thigh down across my chest. Her fat lips fit tightly around me. And we begin to whisper a song to each other; working toward a magic spell.

Moses, she said.

I have no father.

What?

The darkness is not difficult to adjust to. No real estries under here. Only a corner of daylight exploits our darkness from around the edge of the bedpost from the frontdoorway. And yet there is enough light to show a woman how to come out of the wall. She's wearing a helmet with a gold crown. There's a bird head erected from the crown. Its feathers are also gold. The woman has big eyes and she opens her mouth and says: I'VE COME TO REPORT THIS TO YOU. And she suddenly grips the tips of her tits between index finger and thumb and shoots her milk into our faces but it misses our mouths and Uta screams: I'VE GOT SOMETHING IN MY EYE— SEE IF YOU CAN SEE IT!

I try to see into my own eye. Through her eye. I open the eye. A malefic potency, here? There's really nothing there. I can't even see myself looking into my own eyes. I'm conscious that my penis is still, quiet, and still in her. A naked hairy man is walking along a lonely highway from the back of her memory. He's wearing a hat and around his neck he carries a nonprofessionally printed sign: PLEASE READ THIS SIGN PAY ME WHAT YOU CAN   MAY GOD BLESS YOU THANK YOU

But I don't understand. *Pay* for what? Anyway, the woman on the wall vanishes. I didn't see her leave but a witch has replaced her. This female magician carries a thick curved sword and the toes of her sharp shoes jut from under her rusty gown.

I fuck demons, she says, and I've come to sterilize you two sinners!

You talking to me?

Yes, Uta.

You're getting soft, Uta says.

I've put a spell on him, says the demoniac old creature. I used his own excrement mixed with pig and goose turds mixed it in his oatmeal.

My penis slides from Uta's tight wet presence. I start to speak to tell the witch to go away.

Shhhhhhhh, says Uta. I hear Gal coming.

We have the screen door locked and Gal stands there shaking it. She calls the name Moses six times then begins crying.

We lay holding each other, Uta and me, and listening to Gal whimper and suck her thumb.

Locked in or out she cries, I said. In a low voice.

Fuck the little bitch.

The witch, meanwhile, goes back into the wall.

Karo is slender and there's something sticky slimy about him. He is jet black with liver-lips and he hates Gal and all girls.

But he wants to hold my hand and he pulls me into shadows to touch me. He can bite like a dog and he is the one who lives in a house on a hill looking down upon us.

I saw a ghost white go up his gray front steps. I shall never forget it. One of the very first things in life. Perhaps also the last. A child ghost, no bigger than Casper, the Friendly Ghost. And the dogs in the neighborhood began howling, slime dripping between their teeth from their mouths, But that was just as night undressed day and slipped into the cool freedom of the moon.

Karo taught me how to masturbate I think and then I apparently forgot it because later Grew and B.B. taught me again.

I was with Karo and it was a bright morning full of freshness and lazy with silence. Let's hide from the girls, Karo said, as he took my hand into his own. Let's hide where they'll never find us. Gal was jumping rope with a girl named Levite and they were singing *O Lil Liza, Lil Liza Jane! O Lil Liza, Lil Liza Jane!* Karo's home was perched on stilts and we stood up and walked under it beneath the front porch where Karo had erected his own private house.

Have a seat.

He meant for me to sit down on an old car tire where weak sunlight fell through the porch floorboards and the steps created a splatter of light and shadow. What would he talk about? I sat down and wondered. Would it be the immoral practices of Abraham or the Orthodox approach to sodomy or how high the London Bridge stands in relation to the shore? Ah, but how pointless it was to waste the space of the self in such pure obscenity! Shameful is stringent babble.

This is my home, said Karo.

What do you do here?

I try to suck my own thing but I can't get it all in my mouth so let me suck yours all right?

Did you know that I'm the inspector?

Karo laughs. The *inspector*, huh? He laughs again. Well, inspector let me make you feel goooooooooood! Really good! But, Karo said cautiously, you have to suck mine, too! Otherwise it's no good!

His bed was a lean sheet of newspaper spread on the black earth with the signs of his masturbation already upon it. There, I stretched out, instantly felt his pressure.

Oh, Inspector, he said.

He nursed the open endings of my hope. He jerked his entire body in a fit of anxiety. I ran the tip of my tongue around inside my own mouth while I sniffed something like dog sweat.

I can't do it, I said.

Yes you can; you can do it.

But I can't!

Anybody can do it, Karo said, *you* can do it!

No.

Well, just play with it while I do you.

No.

How come?

Cause I'm a girl and I want to go jump rope with the other girls.

You're not a girl.

My friends are girls, I said.

Karo got off me. His voice was thick. If you tell the girls, he said, I'll kill you. Never tell anybody; do you understand?

Where're we going?

To the landowner's, answered Veronica. She had lost weight and was pale, very pale; and she had the sniffles. But I was coughing and had a high fever.

Is Thursday, the housekeeper, expecting us?

She's the landowner, Moses.

Then, the landowner.

I watched the delivery woman wipe a tear from the corner of her swollen eye. Gal was a baby in her arm, asleep. It was all a mystery and there was nothing else to ask. If I looked up I could see the tops of black trees zooming by against the drenched night skyline. The blue was beginning to turn yellow, sunlight coming. Two colors having an intensely fertile intercourse giving the sadness of ourselves a shock of spontaneous green overtone. The man driving the Ford coup had a wrinkled red neck. He had picked us up in a downpour at the barren night station where the Greyhound bus had dropped us at four o'clock in the morning. And now, the contraption wherein we nestled clanged along through the rainy morning, like malnutrition in the guts of an unlucky infant.

The door is there. Here, where my crusty brown hand reaches. The door is white, it is blank, and it has a gold knob. Its knob is polished to a bright finish and the glow from it offers a mirror; yet, I can't see myself. I don't want to see myself. I want to open the door and go out or if I'm already out, go in. But in *to* what, where? or *on* where? What does the door conceal or expose? Wood painted white or it might be metal. It doesn't make any real difference; my fingertips cannot convey to my mind what they touch. I cannot touch my own spirit. I cannot see myself in the mirror of the knob. I am locked outside myself and I cannot stop thinking about it. I cannot stop suffering.

The knob. I touch the knob and it flutters like a broken-winged bird. It breaks against the pressure of my grip, like something swelling in my hand. But suddenly the door opens to something blindingly bright. It is *space*.

> The bright space of a room that is empty, that looms and draws me in; and yet, the room seems to suffer like an animal with legs tied together during the moment of slaughter. The room howls silently; it is too loud. Too empty, too bright. I have to piss and there isn't the slightest hint of a place private enough to shield my guilt, to ease me through the ache of dealing through the tabooed act; there's something about the hypnotizing quietness, the hopeless emptiness, that offers no sanctuary. The dick that juts out from one's body into the burning brightness, in a function so natural as urinating, has, by virtue of the codes and customs one is subjected to, to apologize to the structured myth, like, *Oh, Lord, forgive me, but Jesus, shit, I gotta take a leak!*

I have a weak bladder and I consciously long to overthrow all my Christian hangups! to be equipped with the blessings of no inner pressure ebbing my spirit and psyche, and ultimately to strip naked, body *and* mind, and stroll casually out into wider and wider circles until I cover the world with the beauty of what I have discovered. Yet, the bright room goes on suffering like a helpless creature being smashed back into the harmony of what we called death. Accept the mood of such a place, yet remember, the very style, the tools that force it into you, ends as a lie. But all lies have degrees. Everything goes straight through me, I am like the earth with rivers running deep, deep and dark passages jutting from one ocean away into another. A dungeon still, my flesh is a dungeon, stung, this moment, by the huge throb of this heat, this light. Yet, I have a thing . . . about light.

> How many doors can you open? The door through which I have just come no longer exists. How can I prove that I came through it? *Why*, really, should I want to prove it, and to whom?

Yet, there, at the other side of the room, is the sudden challenge of a *new* door. And though it looks exactly like the one behind me, and might lead to a more restricted area, it remains, at least until I open it, a *moral question* with a promise of what I like to imagine is an ultimate *good!* Realistically, I should pray for my journey toward a stillness, the day when I shall be quiet, and not have to open doors nor dream of a challenge beyond them; but will such a moment in itself be *an offering* or *a sacrifice?*

> I should simply piss forcefully high into the space and watch the splatter of my own rainfall slide across the glossy floor toward no outlet toward no drain and stay even to see the rivulets begin to come back crashing into each other. Fantasy! Meanwhile, the pressures inside mount.

I do not want to be *this way*—it is these words themselves that separate us, that swipe our spirits and weigh us down like cement around the waistline of an underworld victim dropped into monsterous night water.

> Yet, I am afraid *not* to go to the new door. The minute I touch it the knob comes off. Through the hole where its axial was, a pool of blue tarnished light speeds in past me and stabs the opposite wall where the first door vanished.

My first impulse is to stoop, to peep through the circle of light to see whatever is beyond. But I don't!

> I'm still focused on the spot where the light stabs the opposite wall. There, without a smile, is an image of my own face. Slightly different from what I remembered of it. Somehow, looming there, unmoving, it seems a violation of something yet I cannot decide whether that something is *in* me or simply wit*hin* the world, anywhere. And if I could snatch it, recapture it, erase it, where could I keep it, and how could I ever forget it, or pretend that it was never there, outside myself?

I turn away from all the possibilities of the past toward the new room. *It is* a new room, I see through the hole. Initially I cannot believe that it will be as empty, and just as bright and fake-looking as the present one. But this is the impression gained at the narrow, round opening into it. So, I push it, to open it, and I enter it. Not hesitating as much as I suspect I should.

It seems identical to the one I just left. Like it also this one smells like a dying animal, though it looks as if it should be reeking of fresh paint.

Facing me, is another door, with the same kind of knob. What is *this shit? Whose* playing this lightshow game with me? Why am I in this sterile place fumbling with the prospect of taking a piss as though it were a giant problem?

> Anyway, I go on. It's really very simple: you go on or you do not go on. *I* began running, snatching open door after door, and each room was just as quiet, just as empty, just as bright, and just as oppressive. And, I suppose, somewhere in me, there was a certain trust, hope that, at some point, one *would* be different. One may contain soft tones, shade, objects I could touch and thereby establish a rapport with.

I ran, throwing open door after door, and the ache in my groin was explosive. *I gotta find a place!* Veronica will kill me if I wet the floor! No! Veronica left me! Moses left, too! Thursday will punish me, lock me in solitary confinement! or order her right-hand man, John Flower, to fulfill the duty of a prosecutor—beat me to death! perhaps even deliver me to Death Row and finally even to the electric chair, strap my thin arms and legs in it, and throw the switch that fills me with lightning. Perhaps not so unusual an end for one who has an uncomfortable romance with lights.

In the long run the rooms begin to slant.

> Suddenly, each one is different from the next. As I speed through them my eye is snatched and tormented by the various structures that attract it; yet, I can't determine what anything is, and for some reason, now, I don't dare stop until I come to the end.

Finally, I stumble into a room that has a window. Sweat pours down my skin beneath my clothes. At the window, the window glass shows nothing but a solid sheet of blackness. Is it the outside world? It must be night without light; cause who would carve a window onto the unlighted underworld? I press my hands, the tips of my sweaty fingers, my lips, my cheeks, to the cracks of the window, desperately trying to detect *air*. If the window faces the night certainly there should be air and at the same time I'm suddenly aware that oxygen and nitrogen are the elements in here that are scarce. I try to open the window. I push up for a moment or two before I notice that it has no mechanism for mobility. It was made to never open. A dupe. To feed an illusion.

In complete desperation, like a trapped rat, I turn around, piss leaking down my left thigh—since my dick has a habit of resting against its inner cushion—and like in a very moral story, I see that the wall behind me is lined with the kind of urinals you use in public toilets. Why had I noticed the window before noticing the urinals? Or, had they been there, when I first entered the room, and if not, why now, and why in the room where, for a change, there was a window? And why all these fucking stupid questions?

Anyway, I unzipped, but holding my prick, and waiting for the stream to start, I could not piss. I did not *have* to piss. The pressure was still in me though; and I had misunderstood it, since pissing was not the point. Obviously.

Thursday Flower was a tall, bony, coal-black woman with short patchy hair, faded blue eyes, a hawk nose and she wore long loose cheap cotton dresses; *imagine* her, consoling skinny, ghost white, pretty and soft, Veronica!

Anyway she pretty much commanded her section of the prison. But she had help. Her right hand man was John Flower. John was nasty and ugly and vicious. He was dark.

He had a light skinned wife. They called her Lucy "Greenhalge" Flower. She had her problems, too.

Then, there were two others I haven't mentioned often: B.B. and Grew. B.B. used to go around telling people he was a fire-maker. He was as black as Thursday and was short and strong. On the other hand, Grew was tall and skinny and closer to Lucy (Nasteylipp) Flower's complexion. These two boys were real slaves. However, to make himself feel better, Grew, finally gave himself a title: Farmyard Attendant. Now, I don't know how true it is but B.B. said B.B. stood for Butter Butt. Others said it was really Buck Brent. Grew was sometimes referred to as Apple Butt yet his real name, I think, was, George Brent. I never heard much about their guard but their delivery woman was called Sugar Girl—whose real name was Valerie Flower Brent.

A happy black face shouts: THE WAR IS OVER THE WAR IS OVER! HAAAAAAAAAAAAAAAAAAAAAY! from the opened window of a green army truck going by.

And a shower of glossy and colorfully wrapped candy bars is thrown out toward us, flying like helpless baby birds, headed straight for the ground.

Mobile black and white grinning faces going by. Their faces reminded me of the lack of joy in Moses', and in John's, neither of whom had ever been inducted or fought even a segment of a war. No. I take *some* of that back: Moses, once was drafted under the name Fairfaz Shortt, was shipped to basic training, finished, was shipped to some remote frontline, where Negro soldiers were being used as cannon fodder, and Moses froze from instant battle fatigue; and had to be returned to civilian life since, even as cannon fodder, bad luck wasn't interested in falling upon him. And now, B.B., Grew, myself, and even Gal, stood on the side of the highway, barefoot, the long summer grass stroking our legs, bickering, jumping to catch the candy, and trying, at the same time, to keep count of the number of trucks rolling by, coming from, or going to the end or the beginning of peace or violence. Mostly, the black hands throw the candy bars. Sometimes, though, even white hands pitch a candy bar toward us. It is always a rare surprise and the act reduces the distance, the strangeness behind those white faces. (I remember vaguely that Veronica's face was white, but she has been gone so very long now, I wouldn't recognize her if I were to see her.)

I wanna join the army, said B.B., with a mouth full of Baby Ruth. Man! he continued, those uniforms really look great! really cool!

Grew looked sharply at him and said, You crazy, nigger? Don't you *know* people *like us* ain't admitted?!

I could get permission from the warden!

You don't even know the warden's name!

Suddenly, a Butterfinger bar hit B.B. in his forehead. Grew, meanwhile, burst out laughing at the incident, he tapered off, holding the foreskin of his prick for comfort, trying to stop himself from shaking; besides, during his moment of insane release, we were steadily copping the shower of candy bars still flying at us.

If I had been one of the heads in one of the trucks passing I might have seen three male and one female scarecrows with the strange ability to jump about like a monkey and catch flying candy.

All through the night the big slow trucks continued to roll along the highway past Thursday's place. During the night Thursday, who slept in a big white bed, in the same room in which we, B.B., Grew, and myself, slept, snored brashly. Gal slept beside Thursday (John Flower and Lucy Flower, who came for one reason or another to this farm every day, lived and slept in another section of the confinement; John and Lucy had a house in Chickamauga, which is in Lynchburg County. They had to come through Sodacracker Heights out of Remus Road to get to Thursday's place, a farmhouse facing highway 69, across from the "colored graveyard").

In the morning, after B.B., Grew, and I brushed our teeth and offered ourselves as sacrifice (and having survived the offer) we shot out to the highway where the vehicles were still going by. We waved our arms and jumped up and down but nothing happened. The soldiers hardly looked at us. None of them, not even the black soldiers, smiled. And there were no candy bars thrown at us. We stood there all morning, very confused, very hurt. And with stomach aches.

At first it was difficult to make out what the hassle was all about, except that Thursday earlier told John, You need to sleep in a bed separate from Lucy's—that, she said, would solve the problem.

All day John and Lucy had been bickering and it was night now and for some mysterious reason, Grew, B.B., and I had been transported to Chickamauga (having left Gal with Thursday, in the other restricted area. Thursday hardly ever let Gal out of her sight cause she went around all day with this notion in her head that somebody'd play with Gal's twat or something. And naturally, Thursday thought such a thing was a sin); and now we could hear Lucy inside their house shouting at John. Shit like, *Just tell me what in the fuck makes your word so fucking holy? Huh, tell me that, willya?*

Lucy Nasteylipp, drunk from white wine and a black whine, it appeared, had looked through the silk scarf at the moon in a secret and serious effort to try to determine who (if anybody) her next lover man would be. (Lucy had, in her dark historical reference, a kind of General Assembly of illicit lovers that she sometimes approached with the political coolness of one practicing a sort of Good Neighbor Policy.)

So, apparently, John, the Prosecutor, had let his furious jealousy emerge and ooze around on the surface of their rapport (or lack of rapport). We sat on the stoop so we could have clear access to the swollen verbal sounds coming from inside. He screamed about sperm, piss, shit, snot, liquor, and human sweat; he, at one point, accused her of having bedded down with the ol' renegade, Moses Westby, in another town, while Moses was traveling under the elusive name of Gibbon Sambo

29

Eynon and trying to cash a line of bad checks. It appeared that Moses had bragged to the prosecutor once, long ago, about having fucked this certain chick whose face he never saw; the broad had simply stuck her naked ass-end into an opened basement window where Moses was resting for the night. Moses and this woman hadn't said a word to each other; he rammed her, shot his load, and pulled out; and the lady dropped her dress and went away. Well, when John heard this, and when he remembered that Lucy had been in *that* town at *that* time, he knew it *had* to have been her—no other woman on earth could've done that! And while the idea of her doing such a thing excited John it also caused him passionate anger! But there were so many other past incidents he was throwing in her face tonight, trying to wrench from her a confession of obtrusive infidelity.

John was also accusing Lucy of manifesting wet heat with the odd handsome black man called Fisheye. (A gray-greenish eye, just one eye, looked upon the world from Fisheye's disfigured face, made half-sightless by the huge and blunt rage of a warden, a white man now dead. It was said by many inmates and free folks, too, that Fisheye carried the bad luck of a two-dollar bill. It was also said that he was an expert on the *statute of limitations,* that he had taught himself the legal nature of *equity* but hadn't learned shit about asserting personal claims he might have been able to manage. But shit, we were all victims of the *laches!*)

Well.

John came stumbling from the house reeking of the cheap moonshine he'd consumed all day, and Lucy was on his heels screaming, SHIT ON YOU SLICK—! (She called him Slick when she needed to). The Slick prosecutor staggered to his automobile, a T-Model Ford parked alongside the dirt road of Remus Road. We stood and walked out to the edge of the grassy unkept front yard, watched him wheel the vehicle around and drive off, in front of a cloud of dust rising in the light the sun threw on the moon.

Nasteylipp Lucy stood on the edge of her unpainted wood front porch and whimpered in anger.

Grew, she said, come here.

Grew scratched his woolly head and shuffled up to her.

Yes Miss Lucy, Grew said, what can I do fer you? I wants to does any*thang* I kin ta makes you happy. Yo' wish is my command! Heehee!

Don't be silly, Grew, she said, that stupid nigger's gone to get Fisheye. I'm scared.

Among us, Grew was the only one she treated like a human being; and this was the first time I'd ever heard Nasteylipp reveal anxiety or fear. Her voice was shaking, and though I couldn't see her eyes, despite her fury, I suspected she was also close to tears, which, for her, would have been completely out of character. It was just impossible to imagine a hard, big, sensuous, mean-looking bitch like that weeping. I could see her sticking a hot straightening comb up a baby's asshole but shedding tears, holymoses, no, I jes couldn't get to it! the *image,* I mean.

I squatted in the yard, in earshot, and pulled blades of damp grass, and one after another, chewed them thoughtfully. Thursday once said that Fisheye had been, before I was born, a popular minister in various areas of the restricted area. But the landowner also added that Fisheye was a faker from way back! It appeared that his "calling" had been arranged by a District Attorney (white), a Warden (white), the (white) Grand Wizard of the Klub Niggerkill, a secret society (group) operating on very deadly terms in the penal colony known as Chickamauga; and, having made a deal with these local authorities, Fisheye (who, in those days when he sported *two* good eyes, was known by the lofty name, Apostle Maskrey Toft Dingle), proceeded to preach mainly the stifling word of Saint Paul (the weird Jew living in a city where Jews were hardly tolerated years and years ago); and Fisheye fucked-up a lot'a inmate mentalities in his time until he was caught in a broom closet (*uppity nigger!*) having the huge, *un*circumcumcised knobby head of his giant black meatweapon furiously nibbled and crunched by the warden's tiny, delicate, blue-eyed blonde, nineteen-year-old daughter. When the warden caught them Percival was working at Fisheye's thing so passionately she'd almost ripped off the prepuce, and Fisheye himself was whining like a medicant monk in prayer. As it turned out, Percival was a compassionate girl (not just a perfectionist), and she saved Fisheye's life by promising her father (a very hard and cold man who, it was said, descended from Northumberland conquerors in the Old World), now in the uptight New World, that she would end her own life if any harm came to Apostle Maskrey Toft Dingle. Actually, it was the psychic pain of this dilemma that killed the old white racist. It was rumored among local white racists (the larger portion of the population of free folk) that perceptive and pretty Percival fled to New York and married in holy wedlock sixty-nine thousand niggers, one after another, until she couldn't come any more and after that she went about simply spreading spiritual love among black men until she died from the excitement of such a rich and full life. It was his connection with Percival that had *made* Fisheye a local legend. Generally he was known *as* Fisheye but by his closest friends he was called Broomcloset. Kinda ironic, he'd lost one eye that day in the broom closet, and the one that remained looked like a fisheye. The irony, of course, lingers somewhere in the paradox of the two names. But Fisheye, himself, preferred his older more lofty name, yet, even the older inmates who at one time respectfully addressed him by it, had, by now, completely forgotten it.

So.

Now, Lucy, apparently, had had a thing going with this character out of Chickamauga Folklore, and her man, John Flower, was out, rattling and spitting along some road, feeling the sting of yellow jackets and bees in his brain cells, and nursing the taste in his mouth for the enemy's cool blood.

In any case it was probably not more than twenty minutes after John left that we heard him coming back along the dirt road, another cloud of red dirt behind him, in the moonlight, even before the initial one had settled back.

Lucy stepped down from the porch and through her loose dress scratched approximately where the hairs of her vagina were situated. She spoke tensely. Now, I ain't gone let this crazy nigger fool kill *me*. I'm gone run cause I don't know what Slick is likely to do.

Lucy went past where I squatted, chewing grass.

Grew, she said, looking back over her shoulder (while the huge cheeks of her rump shuddered like jello beneath her

32

dress), I can trust you, Grew. I'm gone hide in the cornfield for awhile, okay? *Don't tell 'em nothing!* And don't let these cats open their mouths; and—

> But B.B. cut off her sentence with: What if he beats us to make us talk?

If any of you snitch *I'll* personally castrate you and peel the skin off your fucking faces with a dull razor blade—is that clear?

> But Lucy didn't wait to hear from us whether or not it was lucid. She meant business. She dashed through the grass, clear of the road, to the side of her front yard, crossed the side road, and climbed the embankment—silhouetted a moment against the now cloudy moon—and disappeared among the tall stalks of corn, just as John pulled his T-Model Ford to a clanging stop out front, directly in front of the path to the porch. Obviously he hadn't seen her go. Her escape had been shielded by the trees at the edge of the yard, plus, the angle of his vision and the night in general *or* in particular had been, so far, in Nasteylipp's favor.

There was a man with John. They came up the path together and when they reached the porch it became clear to us that the newcomer was that infamous lover, Fisheye. I was kinda thankful for the night cause Fisheye's empty eyesocket was always difficult to look at; yet I'd never been able to focus on his face without morbidly gazing at the loose skin which he never covered with a traditional patch. (Said he always wanted the world to experience his misfortune and that to wear a patch would mislead the visiting spirits of somebody he called his "holy father" who would avenge him one day, a day he called "judgement day.") (Miscellaneous information had been incidentally picked up while hanging around the prison barbershop, sweeping hair for Mr. Hain Alcock—who, it was rumored, was born without a penis or in any case, did not, now, have one—a factor that endeared him to the local, free white men, including the son of the late Grand Wizard of the Niggerkill Klub, now, headed by this particular male descendant.)

> The moon glowed in Fisheye's naked murky eye as he looked down toward me while John climbed the porch and entered the house, calling, *Where are you, bitch?*

Fisheye stood on the porch until John came back having discovered that his home was minus his woman. John looked down at a sixty-degree angle upon Grew, sitting on and wiggling his nervous legs from the edge of the porch. John didn't speak; I watched his shadowy, narrow, drunk eyes; he seemed to be trying to decide something difficult to come to a decision on. Grew, I'm sure, was achingly aware of the "danger" implicit in John's brooding.

Grew, said John.

Grew looked up. Yes, sir?

Do you believe I could rip all the shingles off the roof of this house with my bare teeth?

Grew began to shudder, more from John's tone than his proposal. Grew believed in machines, morality, money, dreams, insanity and Grew believed in mercy; but he did *not* believe that Mister John "Slick" Flower possessed the capacity to treat him—Grew—justly and kindly. And Grew began to shake even more, finding himself speechless, as he quietly reflected on the strength of John's teeth. Which were huge, uneven, and badly stained not so much from tea, tobacco, nor moonshine, but, primarily from the prosecutor's internal gall.

Fisheye, meanwhile, threw back his head and guzzled the burning brew of the local bootlegger bottled in a used container with a *White Horse* label. His bumpy throat jumped *poco poco*. The moonlight caused his half-closed good eye to sparkle like a ruby half sunk in black mud as the sounds of his throat and the liquid entering him momentarily occupied me. I wanted to keep on dwelling on Fisheye and mystery and peace, and not witness the coming fury of the prosecutor turned loose upon helpless Grew. It had always been too naked and gagging to focus on for long.

Grew still hadn't answered John, and *that* in itself was enough to elicit a whipping. Softer but more menacingly, Slick spoke again. Fuckface, you hear me talking ta ya . . .

Yes, sir.

But beyond "sir" silence fell again, except for the distant howling of some stray or wild dog against the backdrop of the endless crick of crickets. One minute, two minutes.

Then, quieter still, Slick John spoke. Fisheye smacked his lips once but his guzzling had stopped. Slick John was murmuring and no one could hear him. Fearfully Grew begged the prosecutor to repeat himself, which, also was a bad *bad* request. It meant that he, Grew, hadn't been "paying attention," and in the past, that sorta shit had earned him hours and hours of torment and bloodstained pain.

I said, began John, come in the house with me.

Trembling, Grew got up and followed John. Fisheye sat down on the stoop and held the bottle up against the moon to see how much was left.

Wanna sip, kid? he said, looking at me.

No.

Fisheye laughed and swung his attention to B.B., who was leaning against a beam of the porch, legs crossed, and hands squeezed down into his tight bluejeans. Hey, said Fisheye, how about you—? Hoghead, this yella nigger, too good to drink wid me. *Here.* He held the bottle toward B.B. and B.B. shook his head, no, no thank you. So Fisheye himself threw the bottle up to his face and took a long swig.

My knees were aching from squatting so long but I could not conceive of moving. I was frozen in a nightmare where I should run but couldn't. Suddenly, I saw Fisheye stand the bottle (click) on the porch. Sigh. A half yawn; then, lean back on his left elbow, and with his right hand, dig into his pants pocket. He brought out a stiff oblong object that looked like a dead robin. I squinted to make sure; and *it was;* and it was about ten inches long. The light was good enough so that I could see the chestnut-red breast. Well, naturally, it seemed odd that a *grown* man should be carrying around in his pocket such a thing; and yet, somehow I thought I understood it. The only thing that worried me a moment was: what would he do about the possible problem of the tiny pest that lived at the root of the feathers, in the bird's skin. He probably hadn't thought about it, especially if they hadn't yet begun to reach and crawl about on Fisheye's own skin. I looked at B.B. for a reaction but he didn't seem interested in Fisheye's possession. B.B. looked at the thing, then twisted his face the way he does when he's bored; then looked toward the embankment where Nasteylipp was last seen.

I found it impossible to hold back my question. I said to Fisheye, Can I see that?

Sure thing. Come take a look.

My knees cracked as I stood up and inside the house I heard Grew giggle and began laughing. It was good to hear that sound. Maybe Slick John was telling him jokes about the many wild incidents of his experience as a tax collector in the penal colony.

I stood at Fisheye's knees smelling his enormous sweaty odor blended with the stink of the booze I knew what it was, nevertheless, I asked, What is *it?*

It's my bird.

What does it do?

Fisheye didn't answer me because at that moment Slick John Flower came out, the screen door banging behind him. He had his right hand extended before him, palm up, and in it, he had something carefully balanced. I thought it surely must be something quite precious because of the awed expression on his face. His eyes were focused on the . . . it was something oblong but slightly smaller than the bird. Slick John stooped beside Fisheye, and they both began to grin. B.B. slowly drifted over, obviously not wanting to, but to see what was happening. Suddenly it became clear to me, what the object was. I recognized it as Grew's peter.

Isn't it nice? said John.

Here, said Fisheye, put it in.

Fisheye was holding open a deep long slit in the robin's chest and it was obvious that the bird was hollow inside. Carefully, like a surgeon working on a heart transplant, Slick John eased the spongy, shrunken thing down into the crevice, and Fisheye ceremoniously closed the sides over it.

A moment of silence was observed, then Fisheye spoke.
How is he?

Fine, fine. I left him playing with Lucy's straightening comb. He's going to be *just* fine!

> B.B. suddenly started laughing uncontrollably as Fisheye patiently reinserted the bird in his pocket. And at that moment, from the cornfield, we all heard a loud and beautiful, almost sensuous, sneeze!

Me and B.B. ran behind them and it didn't take long for them to catch her and throw her down, breaking stalks of corn in a area of about a thirty-foot radius. It was Slick John's own corn, anyway. Nasteylipp Lucy kicked, bit, scratched, and screamed, but Fisheye and Slick worked at her swiftly and skillfully like two cowboys bringing down a steer in a rodeo. Fisheye, with his own knees, held her legs; Slick, using the same method, held her arms. We stood close. Excited. My throat seemed to contract, almost close. Fisheye and Slick were facing each other and Slick gave the one-eyed man some sort of eye signal, not exactly a wink. But it was undoubtedly a *go-ahead* signal.

> *What're you trying to do to me?!* demanded Lucy.
> She squirmed; her torso bounced and she tried to close her thighs but Fisheye had them firmly stretched like the arms of a compass-drawing instrument.

Okay Doctor Maskrey Toft Dingle, said Slick John, speaking to Fisheye. The one-eyed man's face was alarmed for a moment, then a wide grin broke at the damp edges of his purple lips.

> *Apostle,* he said, sweetly.

He threw up Lucy's dress and the moon glowed on her fat belly. She wore no underclothes; she never wore any underclothes, which is why her thick bush was not a new sight to my eye. I'd seen it many times at times when she stooped to pick up something or sat carelessly in a chair. I often dreamed of her in a way that I was scared to dream of Veronica, though, I had, by accident also seen Veronica's bush a number of times. Such incidents always fascinated me because I never really had had sex with a woman or a girl; and the babysitter episode didn't count as sex and even *then* I knew it.

> Why were they taking so long? I was anxious to see the act. A twig snapped somewhere and the night wind blew softly. The

Fisheye apostle was digging in the pocket where he'd put the bird. But what he brought out was a two-ounce white tube of polymer acrylic; holding it between the shaking thumb and fingers of his left hand, with the other he upcapped the pigment, and squeezed a little up from the airtight tube. For a moment my eyes shifted to Fisheye's tense face: he was nervously chewing his bottom lip. His dimples showed dimly. Nasteylipp twisted and cursed and Slick John groaned impatiently. Fisheye shifted the tube now to his left hand and squeezed it; I watched it emerge snakelike, glossy and red, onto the tip of his right index finger. Satisfied with about an inch of it out, he ceremoniously began to smear it into the thick matted hairs around Lucy's hole.

Shit, Fisheye, snapped John Slick, that's not *enough!*

Nasteylipp Lucy screamed, HELP!

Scream all you want, said John, call the Governor of Chickamauga, if you wanna, call *anybody!* Nobody can help you!

Meanwhile, Fisheye had squeezed out a much longer portion of it and was vigorously applying it to Lucy's nappy nest.

The stuff drys fast, said Fisheye, *too* fast!

Slick John barked impatiently, *Just work faster!*

And a moment later Fisheye was done. He leaned back and looked squintingly sideways at the painted cunt. Appraising his work like a real mastercraftsman.

You finished?

Yeah, John. And she's as beautiful as a shark.

Let me up! shouted Lucy.

And the two men turned her loose; she jumped up and shook herself like a dog does. We stood watching her, her wrinkled dress now covering the painted twat. Her face was puffed up with anger and her lips were pulled back tightly as though she were about to make a hissing sound. Slick John and Fisheye remained on their knees, looking up awesomely at her.

Elegant, said Fisheye, and as rare as a frog with the mumps! Yeah, said Slick John; she looks just like a cinnamon tree. Let's go have a drink to her.

She was fuming and stamping her feet and tearing tortuously at her own garment as the two men were hugging each other and laughing. By the time they reached the edge of the corn-field they were singing some song the words of which we could not clearly hear.

It was a pale orange truck with a light blue canvas top to its back section which was its mobile all-purpose store.

> There it comes! shouted Thursday, from the garden, where she was on her knees, weeding her tomatoes.
> GET OUT IN THE HIGHWAY AND STOP THAT TRUCK!

She hadn't addressed any one in particular. Having all grown up with a penal psychology we all feared cruel and unusual punishment almost always so we all ran to fulfill the command. Almost knocking each other down. Jumping, shouting, and waving our arms. Grew was the tallest, and possibly the strongest, so he commanded the center of the highway, facing the approaching vehicle, going through his frantic motions.

> The truck pulled to the side of the highway and stopped in front of the landowner's place. We cautiously circled it, eying the big, redfaced, redneck, redheaded guy who stepped bluntly down from the cab. The cab squeaked, seemed to have been made of not metal but some sort of dense testtube plastic. He was about five feet over the tallest of us, and when he spat the nasty dark-green wad of shit that he'd been churning in his jawls, tongue, and teeth, it flew directly over our heads, splattered against the delicate face of a loud red rose on one of Thursday's favorite rosebushes.

Hi'ya boys, the truck driver groaned.

> Gal snickered, *knowing she* wasn't a boy, and obviously now suddenly aware that the big blockheaded white man had to be a goon.

B.B. and Grew answered the man politely. We fine, sir, they said. With as much awe as one might expect to witness displayed before officers of the State Department of Corrections! I knew he wasn't J. Edgar Hoover but I couldn't figure the dude out, so I said nothing; and Gal was openly laughing at him. He *was* a funny creature!

The truck driver squinted his eyes. Where's that ol' black gal, Twat? Oh, there she comes! Out there in the garden. Sure would like to get her in solitary confinement just once for twenty-four hours! *Hehe*—!

Then his eyes snagged on me, unable to pull away.

Ain't seed you here before, boy. The gal, neither. His lips hung; he was waiting for me to respond. I wasn't going to but before I could Grew spoke. They come from another area.

What's the name of your area? asked the bloated red face. I couldn't take my eyes from his face, and I couldn't speak.

Into the silence, the truck driver spoke again. I'm a *white man;* boy, can't you see I'm a white man? . . . I used to be a parole officer and handled a lot of capital offenders. My brother-in-law is an officer in the Administration of Justice. I may not be a parole officer any longer, boy, but I'm still a *white* man—Now, I'm gonna ask you again: where you come from . . . ?

I don't know the name, I confessed.

Every place's got a name.

I know that, I said.

Can't you say *sir* to a white man? the truck driver said.

Yes.

Well, say it.

Say what?

You know what, nigger! I SAID SAY SIR TO ME!

For the most part, I had no clear notion of what a "nigger" was; and, for the lesser part, his calling me one didn't convince me that *I* was one. Plus, I was scared and when fear has me my heart belongs to it—and hardly to anything else. So, I was speechless.

The big redhead snatched a handfull of my curly hair and yanked it, throwing my skull back, almost snapping my neck;

41

my eyes turned upsidedown. He held my face at the chin with the big meaty paw of his other hand. The monster was looking down, directly into my eyes. In his, I saw the reflection of the Devil.

It gave me faith, and a sort of strength I had not before known to be in my possession.

Cat got your tongue, nigger?

Your mama, I said.

Boooooooy, he said, aren't we brave!

He slapped me then spat in my face. Before I could recover from the slap, I felt the tip of his shoe stab my belly and knock the breath out of me. My head slammed against the brick wall surrounding the flower garden before the house. The wall was actually only about a foot and a half high and when my head cracked against it, I was practically on the ground. Before I passed out I felt his shoe once again rip the flesh from the area above my ear where my hairline begins.

When I came to, there was a blond wig hanging on one side of my head and I was being held up in front of a mirror. The truck driver was holding my shoulders and he was grinning. I tried to spit in his face but it landed on the mirror; some of it ran down the front of my shirt. I took in the scene quickly. He had me sitting atop a footlocker inside the mobile store. Some distance back in the mirror stood Thursday, obviously scared half to death. She was actually trembling. Imagine it! Big badass Thursday, the landowner! She, who'd rip off my balls with her butterknife, now, stood shaking in fear of this ex-parole officer in a white skin who was degrading and brutalizing me; and she, apparently, was really helpless to defend me.

Look at yourself, the man said.

He shook my shoulders.

Look! he commanded.

But I refused to keep my eyes opened.

He slapped me and I spat again at the mirror and this time he realized what I was trying to do.

It made him twitch.

42

Before I could close my eyes again I felt the heavy metal hardness of his hand rip my face.

I saw a huge red splash—blood. It enveloped me and I passed out.

Blank.

You're a cute nigger, boy, she said.

Leave the kid alone, bitch, said her husband.

The flies, dead, on the flypaper hanging from the ceiling. The night-absence of their buzzing. The screened porch, the yellow electric light over the front door. I cannot *hear* buzzing if I *think* there is no buzzing. Bugs hum like dumb beggars at the pores in the skin, the rusty wire.

He is white, she is white, they are white.

I don't know what to do with my hands. My eyes are restless. My face, my arms, my legs are restless.

Their words, their voices. Like the truck driver, they too, are more famous, more powerful than us. They never get caught through the tongue by fishhooks while innocently swimming. Never see their own blood flow downstream behind while somebody tries to land them. He once worked for the Rehabilitation Center, says Thursday; but now is employed by a committee designed to investigate the nature of precipitated homicide. She, his drunk wife, according to Thursday, prior to coming here, was once employed by the Research Committee on Life Imprisonment. (What can Thursday herself brag about except being the landowner and the housekeeper in a very limited area?)

I watched Thursday for my cue.

Her crusty black hand pushed the hot iron back and forth over the cloth. The board, squeaking. The tight clench of her dry, thin lips.

Her eyes do not meet mine.

44

Now, what's wrong with telling him he's cute?

Your style, said the shabby white man to the shabby white woman. It's your fucking style, bitch!

The pale shabby woman, sitting in the straw chair, lifts the cup of beer to her face, again. Her eyes, sparkling red. Her yellow hair, like corn hair, hangs stringy to her shoulders. I watch her tired, unhappy eyes, the jumpy skin over their bulbs. She smiles to herself.

Well, he *is* cute.

The man was stretched out on the swing, motionless, his head sunk in the nest of three pillows of faded cotton.

. . . And he looks straight at you, too. Bold, bright eyes. What's your name, honey?

The man spoke for me. His name is Nat Turnips. Why don't you go inside? You've had one too many.

Remember, said the woman, when we had to sneak and drink this shit, Dischel?

Don't call me Dischel, said Dischel.

Her teeth were long and yellow like a dogs'. Shit, she said, you still call me Papanek as though you were still at the Human Relations Center.

Officially I am, bitch, and don't you forget it.

Yes, Dischel. You go right on, teach your white control, your American Democracy, self-renewal, consciousness expansion, the joys of the male dilemma and the misfortune of the female quandary!

You know that's not what the Human Relations Center is all about, Dischel said, with a groan, shifting the weight of his body in the swing.

Thursday's iron made a squeaking sound, apparently, on silk.

This lost art form that Thursday is demonstrating right now, for example, said the shabby man, is one of the aspects of human experience we're looking into. It's why I asked her here tonight . . .

Well, said Papanek, with a laugh, you certainly could've fooled me! I thought we hired her to do our ironing cause we're too fucking lazy to do it ourselves!

Dischel turned helplessly toward Thursday. Thursday, he said, you know I'm the head of the Human Relations Center, don't you?

Yes, sir, I heard *some*thing about it.

Before speaking again the shabby man drank from his dark bottle of beer. Now, he spoke. At the Human Relations Center we simply try to teach other whites as much as possible about nonwhites.

Papanek coughed and spat some beer on the floor. Blue veins stood out on her neck like barbed wire under tight cellophane. It sounded unnatural and Dischel gave her a dirty look. He actually sneered.

But he went on, addressing himself to slaving Thursday. We try to make possible a white interchange of thought, he said.

Meanwhile, I was hugely thankful they'd turned from me. If only I could now disappear; but I was held here by tacit committment, as Thursday's assistant, her runner. I felt about as hopeful as a nigger accused of rape in 1938 in Mississippi who has been promised Clarence Darrow as a Defense Attorney. In subcultural terms, that would put you in a sort of mental middle land, as opposed to rock bottom or high land.

. . . and we provide an outlet and storehouse for stimulus and knowledge about *your people,* Thursday.

You don't know nothing about *my* people. Thursday laughed to soften her rebuttal.

Come here, Nat, Papanek said to me.

The man sighed painfully.

Thursday tightened her tight lips tighter.

I was standing near the outer wall of the house slightly behind Thursday, still imagining that she might be a shield. When her busy arm went one way, her dress tail flapped another.

In self-defense I pressed my lips tightly together.

Here, said Thursday, speaking to me, go put this cold iron on the coals and bring me the hot one.

Words led people into more words. I understood Thursday's words. I took the iron by its handle, glad for the chance to escape. The iron was quite heavy and I was very weak and thin, frail and small. I right away nearly dropped it on my own toe, as usual. When in the past I'd dropped it on my foot, during the most intense moment of the pain, I always saw the face of the Christian god. A halo glowed around his head and he held his heart in his hand, smiling at me. I wasn't anxious to ever again see the dude.

As I went toward the screen door the shabby woman called Papanek smacked her lips. You could hear her slide her tongue across the outer rim of her mouth. That sound frightened me. It was like wet sandpaper against sandpaper. I thought of Veronica.   Was she somewhere also licking her pink *pink* tongue? I opened the door with my knee and descended the three wooden steps carefully. Into the night, its drizzling rain over and around me. Cricket cricket cricket.

The hot irons are on a wire rack suspended over a low burning fire surrounded by bricks. The whole affair is beneath a roof on four beams, protected from the rain. Just for such an occasion someone once had this idea in the sunlight, possibly at noon?

Papanek's naughty laughter ripples across the night.

I stand close to the fire; yet, the deep coldness, the rain too, seeps into the area around my bones. I ache. I am lonely. Tears well up in my eyes as I place the cold iron over the fire and, holding the stretched-out coat hanger at its end, I drag the hot iron to the edge of the rack.

The flame is sky blue and butter yellow. It also has orange in it. This, against the black blue of the wet night. The moon, obscure, moves silently behind night clouds, like something unnatural, even artificial. But I like the moon because it baffles man—it's not functional. It promises nothing. I swallow the thing inside that had started the tears. Now   I go back across the wet grass holding the hot iron in the hook of the hanger and listening to it sizzle.

Just as I reached the door I heard a scraping sound from a corner of the yard near the fat fig tree. I squinted in the light from the porch and saw a large cage; and in it a large animal was standing on its hind legs; its front legs were against the bars. The moment curiosity gripped me, I shot a glance in through the screen at Thursday, Dischel, and Papanek. For the moment I remained unnoticed. So, I quietly sneaked across the yard to get a closer look at the creature.   The thing was a man—a white man, with dark hair all over his body; and he'd obviously just taken a shit. The odor. And he was trying to cover it with his foot by scraping sawdust over it. He reached his hand through the bars to try to touch me. Raindrops fell on it and looking at his wet fingers he began to grin. I turned away, feeling it would be pointless to make conversation. What, for example, could *he* tell me that I didn't already know? Or vice versa.

The screen door slams behind me. Thursday shouts: *Go back close that door like you got some sense!* I start to give her the iron. But she says, Take it with you! Papanek, meanwhile, says, Shame, shame, a nigger with no manners, shame, shame!

I was thinking of the man out in the cage. Strange, though, to ask any of them about him, never occured to me. They couldn't tell anything that he could not have told me.

A cowbell rang a few times through the rain. When it stopped, the silence was even heavier.   I opened the screen door and stood just inside of it, watching Thursday's face that, in this light, had turned close to the color of copper at its (63.54) melting point.

Go *all the way* outside, boy, and come in again!

In turning, I burned my arm, said, *Ouch!* and outside, in the pivot to come back, after touching the top step, I almost fell backwards. (Once I fell backwards down ten separate flights of stairs. My head bounced, hitting each step; yet, it was as painless as falling down a hillside covered with autumn leaves in the insane safety of a dream.)

Papanek was laughing and Dischel said, You're drunk; can't you drink without getting drunk?

48

I'm no drunker'n you. One thing, I never passed out in public in Jackson City. Put that in your pipe and—

That's *enough,* bitch!

My fingers sweat. I hold them against the screen door (as it closes) until it no longer moves. The spring at the top shudders at the end, and then it, too, no longer moves.

When I held the iron up to Thursday she said, Land sakes, it's probably cold now. She was silent a moment; wet her middle finger, touched the iron, the spit sizzled. She sighed. And without another word on the subject, she began to demonstrate her art again.

I brushed my hands together and fell (sick) against the wall, looking up at the dead flies stuck to the flypaper, smelling the dead wet wood of the porch, the wet chicken shit, dog turds and the mysterious odor of leaves and grass, beyond the porch, all, mixed with the scent of smoke from the fire and shit from the man's cage. Close, however, the sour smell of beer and scorched cloth whipped against my senses. It was all very skerry. Papanek's head, from my angle, looked like a perfect rhombohedron. It almost cheered me!

For comfort I tried to focus my mind on Veronica. Right now Veronica was turning over in her bed. She was asleep and she was dreaming of me. She was sleeping in a glass bedroom in a glass house and tomorrow I'd send a note of love to her attached to the wing of a butterfly. The butterfly would simply know on his own how to get there with the message.

Meanwhile Papanek was saying to me, Can I *feel* your hair? It look *so soft* for nigger hair.

Tears are running down my cheeks. And I hear Thursday urging me: Let the nice lady touch your locks—*go on!*

My barefeet stumble over themselves in my hesitation.

Papanek suddenly leaps up and spills her beer as she grabs me.

She plows her right hand through my woolly hair.

She stinks like poor whites who've been chopping in the fields.

But she giggles as she attacks me and her bloodshot eyes dance in her skull. Her loose slits seem to ooze beer.

49

She is foaming at the mouth and making a goo-goo sound. Her spit falls on my nose and the back of my hand.

I feel a crazy pounding under my skull and a wild, frantic need to run, yet somewhere in me something else is happening. It is a feeling that is thin and creepy, like the beginning of morbid lust.

Then it happens.

Tears shoot from my eyes and I sob beyond control. I start shaking like a paralytic.

Grew was still out deep in the dark woods howling. He sounded like a mad dog. I sat on the back-porch steps of Thursday's house, listening and watching John Flower stumble around in the yard swinging his belt blindly and cussing furiously under his breath. If only he could get his hands on Grew's neck he (John) would break it; or if he could just get close enough to the goddamn sonofabitch he'd cut his (Grew's) ass open. But now, John Slick Flower, carrying out his duty as prosecutor, had not the courage to venture down into the night woods, despite the fact that it was famous only for small game and a harmless brown bear or two once a century? It was not even, in part, a question of whether or not the woods was out of John's penal jurisdiction. Even with the consent of the State Department of Corrections, the Senate Judiciary Committee, the United States Bureau of Prisons, and the United Nations, I doubt seriously if the slick Flower would have set foot below the backyard after nightfall. We all feared demons and since somewhere in himself Slick knew he was a rotten motherfucker and that he couldn't legislate safety nor everlasting life his fear of ghosts very probably was much larger than Grew's—who, on the other hand, had had to decide between *death by the belt* or take his chances in the endless mystery of the woods.

WOOOOOOOOOOOOOOOOOOOO! howled Grew; WOOOOO-OOOOOOOOOOOOO! When the howling stopped Slick shouted down into the damp blackness: YOU THINK YOU HAD A BEATING BOY IF YOU DON'T COME OUTA THEM WOODS YOU GONE FIND OUT WHAT A REAL BEAT-ING IS!

Echo.

Then silence. Cricket cricket cricket . . .

Suddenly, the screen door slammed and nosey Nasteylipp came out and stood behind me. She wasn't speaking to me when she said: Grew is going to wake up the dead wid all that fucking noise!

Grady Flower (at one time a sexual partner of Thursday, and the now-lame other half of her "throne") shouted from his bedroom (which was his only room). What he said wasn't clear so Nasteylipp stepped around me, stood on the top step, pressed her face against the rusty screen of the window to old man Grady's room and inquired: What'd you say, sir? A spasm of coughing then, the paralized old man shouted again: *It's time for the Resurrection of the Dead! It's high time!*

Nasteylipp cleared her throat. I wanted to move, but was afraid to do so: she might take my movement as an insult. (And, of course, that's exactly what it would be!) Nasteylipp looked down on me, sightless; then, out at her mate staggering around swinging his belt in the yard. A few sleepless chickens in the barn were clucking. When the cackling hens stopped their shrill broken cries, in those spaces and in the spaces between Grew's howling and the snap of Slick John's belt back upon itself the active night silence was, despite the everlasting crickets, too terrible to endure, to *have* to endure. Especially with this woman standing over my head. The things that happen below the level of speech are like real with the atomic weight and energy of radioactive isotopes. (Absolutely nothing compassionate or even slightly ingenue about Nasteylipp Lucy! She couldn't be topped and I knew it. She'd done it all, seen it all, and by this late date, knew it all. You could tell by the rhythms of her sentences, even if, like me, you couldn't believe Nasteylipp; in her early years she had, at one time or another slept with an improbable and utterly wild assortment of "types." A few come to mind: A New York German-American manufacturer of turtle saddles, an American-Chinese gravedigger, a Japanese-American pop singer, a Puerto Rican classical pianist, an Irish shoeshine boy, a Mexican senator, an American Indian [Gay Head of Martha's Vineyard] who was president of some bank, a Jewish garbage collector, an Armenian loudspeaker magnetizer, an Occom chief of police from New England, and a lesbian Jewish mother who couldn't cook. Who, in his right mind, would tangle with someone with that kind of record?) So, I sat there, and ached.

At least Grew, down in the woods, could turn to . . . maybe to Adam and Eve or somebody for comfort. In any case, he had the friendly night's aroma—if he could live with it. It didn't necessarily have to be evil and skerry.

And if he really got uptight he could even call on the moon. There might be some comfort in that, if his timing was right.

I betya you're going to chop wood next time Thursday ask you to! shouted John.

Grew howled again.

Blast yo' ass! Slick John cried.

WOOOOOOOOOOOOOOOOOOOOOO!

John Slick stood there in the yard growling and grumbling to himself.

Nasteylipp went down into the backyard and with hands on sexy hips stood in front of Slick. Her speech was an undercurrent.

They chuckled together. Slick's chuckle was perhaps closer to a growl.

The moonlight caught their teeth. The gold in Nasteylipp's mouth glittered sharply. I didn't want to be here—so why wasn't *I* in bed sleeping? What "burden of proof" of my own guilt . . . was I living with in this sleepless imprisonment?

I remember the beating Grew got a few moments ago: The huge belt cut through Grew's blue deniminum arms and back. In the nightlight the blunt wet pendulous bloody streaks stood out on his flesh. Slick is grunting and hissing and swearing as he jumps around, moving in a circle, holding Grew by one hand, and lashing into him with the other. It's like a night dance to the starlight. And he doesn't release the farmhand until he's beat the shirt off his (Grew's) back. And when the ritual was over Thursday (who was standing on the back porch watching) said: I ask him way this morning to chop some wood and I ain't seen no sign of it yet. And before she finished her un-grammatical indictment Grew had stumbled off into the cool safety of the woods.

Few things fascinated me more than watching Grew when he *did* cut wood for the stove fire. The ax blade always fell where he aimed it. He was better at that sort of thing than B.B. and me. Shoot, I couldn't even lift one of them heavy axes over my head without wobbling. But Grew would gototown! WHACK/WHACK/WHACK/WHACK/ steady and precise. And Grew usually had the wood for the day (each day) cut by the time Slick's rude clanging motor clicked off on the left side (of the house) driveway.

Grady Flower was a shrunken old man dying. He'd been dying for years. Grady had become chair-ridden years ago after surviving a strange paralyzing stroke. It was assumed that he'd lost all sensation in muscle function from his hips down. It had happened quite suddenly one hot day while he was on the roof of a church he had designed and built. He was giving his crew some last-minute instructions when the nerve disease (if that's what it was) took him. He fell off the roof and broke an arm. A paralytic, he also had a slight case of paralysis agitans—he constantly shook. And when it rained his muscles, the ones still functional, ached worse than ever.

When it rained I spent a lot of time building mud houses. It was a very profitable business, in a sense. For myself, mainly. I put them on the open market from time to time but nobody ever purchased any.

I thought about Veronica a lot but I couldn't clearly remember her face, her eyes, how her mouth moves or how her long fingernails sound when she scratch her legs through her stockings. I still remembered how she and Moses disappeared and came back—many times; so, maybe this amounted simply to a longer disappearance. I couldn't remember the pain of having had pneumonia. I couldn't remember when Gal was a dance instructor since she was now a spy. I remember always how the light fascinated me but I don't always recall so well. I remember pissing in my pants and I also remember the angel's bride. I'll never forget the sound, the softness of Veronica's voice when she sang when she was unhappy or angry. Nor those bright, empty rooms, and the "nothingness" of where they led. Anyhow, I'm sure I remember better hants at dusk than *being* the secret prince in my own dreams.

B.B. Grew, and I went deep into the wet forest. We saw a huge brown bear slowly moving silently uphill. Tree buds snapping beneath our barefeet. *Holy Talking Bones!* exclaimed B.B., in a whisper, when he spied the creature.

I wonder where he came from? said Grew.

To hell with where he came from, said B.B.

We crouched quietly watching the mammal move.

My arms were hampered by the profusion of undergrowth, fat bushes, and I smelled the wet mustiness of a rabbit's nest near. But we were huddled in a beautiful spot. The floorbed was littered with leaves of alder, baldcypress, butternut, redbud, redwood, sassafras, and things I don't know how to name. A crisp, tan funny-shaped leaf stood between my big and longest toe. It felt funny.

I felt intensely . . . *intensely how?* Like I had a secret, a very valuable secret that I was sharing with Grew and B.B.

Everything in me was beyond shock, I think. For the moment, anyway. It was a breathless moment, filled with life that faces the possibility of death. There was an undercurrent of violence but it was reasonable, natural, life-giving violence.

Grew hissed as the bear paused. The bear was working his nose in the air.

B.B. jumped at the chance to scold Grew. He told Grew, *Sssssh!*

Somewhere in a nearby tree a woodpecker started suddenly drilling a hole.

I watched the bear's response to the woodpecker's noise: he took it in his stride.

Also somewhere nearby bees were buzzing.

A butterfly drifted overhead, floating on the wind. There was an army of black round bugs crawling up a stalk possibly to challenge the butterfly and bees for the juice of the cool flowers. I would turn back to the bear but for the moment I didn't want to do more than notice specks of things. Little disconnected pointless things.

God, said B.B., he's a big bastard!

Wow! I wondered out loud.

Is he male or female? whispered B.B.

The bear was moving again, uphill, passing between trees. A soft mover. You couldn't hear his padded footfalls crushing debris; and we were holding our breath.

Grew holds out his hand against B.B.'s chest and his left against me somewhere near my neck. This is his way of telling us to shut the fuck up.

I glance at the side of Grew's face.

His lips are tight. That's what he want us to do: press our lips tightly together, like that.

Beyond Grew I see B.B. His eyes are blinking in excitement.

I can smell our young body sweat. I wonder how I got here, how long I will last. Where I'm going. Where anybody's going.

Where is the bear going? Does he know?

He stops again; examines a tree.

The woodpecker has started again and the reality of the situation hits me: a SPEECHLESS THING is creeping along only a few inches away and it is, it can be deadly! yet I'm not afraid.

The sunlight scatters down through the trees onto the bear making him look like a thing set afire!

I thought about the man in the cage by the fat fig tree. I *dreamed* about him that night after seeing the bear. He was howling and he had Papanek's face.

Some of you don't trust nor believe in the reality of "the I." I know. Even as Moses Westby or Nicodemus or Nat Turnips. I'm sure it's not my fear. It very well may be my age: any age I happen to be is not human-worthy. I survive anyway with the help of certain natural things like the sun's immutable constancy, its supreme riches, glory, spirituality, its illumination, vanity, idealism, divine eye of wisdom, and heroic image *in* me. But I don't really care. Simply trying to get myself together, maybe even one day get *out*side. As I am born, as I begin to exist, as my birth moves through Aquarius, as the West moves through Aquarius, as Saturn dangerously and moodily moves through Pisces, ruled by a distant Jupiter, my heart and my mind spins through and around the corners of my own spirit, dash and whip like Lake Michigan wind from one end of the alley of the urban mind to the other. Yeah. I have a nature that is idealistic, which puts an edge to my streak of orginality, investing me with at least one moment on earth of intelligence, a detached attitude, driving me beneath shelters of the self. I'm unconventional, eccentric, but I frighten no one. I play alone now. Who could ever play with these cruel motherfuckers surrounding me? They can't even *see* me when they look at me. I'm beginning to hate them. Yes, I *have* to hate them before I can be free. But I can't hate consistently. Sometimes I fall back, being nice. Maybe cause I have some "good" trine planets, some promise that I will not die, that my "death" and crippled spirit will break, that I will recover, because Uranus in Taurus tells me so. Because the Bible tells me so. Sometimes I strike out in many directions at the same time because of the presence of Jupiter in Capricorn. I also know the hot lusty trip of Mars in Libra. I can't forget it because of the Moon's romance with Virgo. Awareness. But what could be lovelier than Mercury in its natural sign, Gemini? But my Sun in Aquarius is also influenced by the Gemini decanante. Hang on to that, like to wet grapes. My ruling spirit, Saturn, leaves me behind prison bars, of the psyche, insecure. I am often left like a blinking light on a distant lighthouse in the fog of a strange shore. Everything is so painfully new, and remains so: like the shock, the intensity of the names forced on me. How it is so mutable, fixed or watery from one moment to the next. Remember how I am born, for you shall know my death, how they all have trapped me in the center of my own luck. Venus in Sagittarius, mutable. And in the strongest of all signs, Scorpio, the Moon brings me tenderly to my knees, with loving care. Yet, I am nearly blind and totally helpless from stupidity. My own lack of air, my imprisonment, grows heavy in my spirit. How can I handle Jupiter in the air spaces of Capricorn? or the Moon, sluggish, there, also, ten days after I begin in North America, Greenwich Mean and Sidereal times. But they gonna ease up, baby, digit.

Thursday is schooling us. When in front of company, she says, if you have to fart just kinda slyly pull the cheeks of your ass apart.

Like this, Thursday?

Yes, Gal, that's it, that's it! Yes, Thursday went on, cause farts are sinful things. Ghosts even hide in farts. That's why they smell the way they smell. Notice the odor of your fart, Gal. It hasn't gone away *yet*. It's because spirits like to stay close to the bodies of living people, listening to their conversation.

Are the spirits the *whole* fart or just part of it?

No, Moses, they just dwell *in* it.

Can you photograph a fart?

No, Moses, you cannot photograph a fart. Sometimes, though, you can take a snapshot of the ghost that gets outa one.

Phew! said Grew. That's a mean ghost Gal turned loose!

Nasteylipp, now, comes out of the house onto the back porch where we are sitting at Thursday's feet, like she was our guru or something. Nasteylipp just stands quietly watching and trying to pick up on the conversation.

> I wanted to know more. I said, But how about Christ, remember that girl who worked down the road for white folks? She said her brother took a photograph of Christ standing in the garden, right behind her and she didn't believe it until the picture was developed and she saw him, with her own eyes, right there, glossy and white and spiritual looking, *right behind her in the picture!*

It was probably a trick, said Nasteylipp. I ain't saying God or Christ don't make visits to the earth but why on earth would he come down and stand in a picture, and get snapped, behind that silly little nigger gal, huh?

> My name is Gal, too, said Gal.

Bless you, honeybunch, said Thursday, and hugged Gal.

> Did somebody just fart? asked Nasteylipp.

Yeah, said B.B., laughing, it was "honeybunch."

> We laughed as much as we dared as long as there was a touch of amusement on Thursday's face.

Little lady, said Nasteylipp, your poots stink worse than a man's. What've you been eating?

> Us? said Grew.

What'd you say, boy? snapped Thursday, menacingly.

> I mean, was Lucy comparing Gal with us. That's what I said, it's what I meant.

Make sure it's what you meant, said Thursday.

Later. We were all sitting on the *front* porch in the dark. The sky was filled with stars. And there were the crickets as usual. The occasional car or truck that swooped by made animals dance from the front-yard tree limbs against the planks of the sad, unpainted house. Strange how those forms refused to look like tree limbs! I saw myself playing cowboy or being a real cowboy stretched out in the front yard, shot through the heart, bloody. My rifle still in my hand, my shotgun still in the bag on my horse that stood still, waiting for me to wake up from death. And my finger still on the trigger. And my ten-gallon hat crumpled in the dust but still on my head. My cowboy boots were untarnished, not a speck of mud on me anywhere! And Grew, with Nasteylipp's camera (a Brownie!) ran out and snapped a picture of me. I was dying already to see what it'd look like—if Christ would be standing in the background! like a silent ghost, against the shadows of the house, especially with all those night beasts jumping against the wall! Slick John sat on the brick step, looking down into his dark fists, and his breathing silence punctuated each of my heavy heartbeats.

Grew very carefully relieved his bowels in a plastic bag and hung the shit neatly all tied up with a string from the limb of a tree near a path through the woods.

Now, he said, all I gotta do is pray.

We knew what he meant, what he hoped for. One day the string that held the bag would be ready to break from age, from rot, and the shit would then drop. On that day, if Grew's prayer was answered by whoever he prayed to, Slick John would

61

be walking along that path and his head would get drenched with a bag of old shit.

> Actually, the *next day* the shit was gone. Birds had pecked their way into the bag to eat the supply of custard and walnuts. On the ground, a brown splotch also covered the twigs and leaves and dead grass.

Until now, because the world's favorite trade is in slaves while it throws long bright shadows against fierce walls, I have snuck in infuriated corners of myself. I still may have to do it. Things, except in my mind, ain't changed *that* much. Slick's thick leather belt, for example, just the sight of it, scares shit out of me. Up the road a piece Sodacracker Heights emits evil white spirits that deck the darkness we struggle beneath. While we kill each other they sing sweetly to each other on Sunday in church. You know what I mean? Its like, anytime, even on the brightest day, it's always gonna rain—*any minute now!* heavy hard rain that while it may be good for corn and potatoes growing it washes half the fucking countryside down into the dry riverbeds. It's just a thing in the air: a kinda disaster nobody can define, yet it's forever present, a pest, but worse.

Slick has a long strip of dried and processed animal skin out and he's slapping and pounding it against the bleached afternoon—*no,* early evening gray shadows. Are we gonna eat it, I want to ask but don't dare! We're in the back yard. It's always that way; *if* you're not in the front yard you know where it's at. Not far away, in Sodacracker Heights, I can hear Dischel beating Papanek over the head with a skillet, and calling her all kinda mean, nasty thangs. It's the life style not only for the slaves but for the free folk, too!

> This is an extreme, unusual moment. Slick sits down, his ass flat on the ground, while he handles the skin. B.B., Grew, Gal, and I stand around him, watching. He says, When I married Lucy I picked her up and carried her across my threshold into my house. Now, I wonder why I'm always doing things like that just because somebody else done it.

Slick John sounded like he was talking to himself. He certainly didn't expect a comment from any of us. None of us second-class prisoners were qualified to speak as an equal with him. *Nosirree!* Looking at him, I wondered for the first time if Slick had a mother and if he'd ever slept with her. Slick's dumb eyes were a motionless, murky yellow with streaks of strawberry red naked swimming in them. They were unshielded arcs made by some welding rod of the booze-drinking spirit!

Later. Down at the hogpin, we hung on the fence, watching. It's hog-killing season. The fat hog eats slop slowly, unaware of his coming death. Slick throws his booted foot on a plank in the fence, props the firearm properly against his shoulder blade, aims carefully. His Winchester, just as the red sun goes down, glows. Suddenly, the blast fills the late evening. One thin, high squeal from the hog and after he makes a short zigzag run he turns over, legs shooting out sideways, shudders, a rivulet of blood pumping out of his skull. The crack of the rifle still sounded in my ears. Slick pulls the trigger again, another hole appears in the hog's head and its shuddering ends. The blood continued to pour out of the skullbone and now began running from its mouth. The bullet really had the character of a 14th-century French Devil: everybody knows he can hit home with deadly force but nobody ever sees him.

> That thin, high deadly sound comes close to breaking through the thin-walled and light-boned area of the skull so neatly that it drives you into an endless but sharp and hot moment of deep *un*responsive psychosis where you are left horrified at the prospect of your own End, coming at you from some far corner of the Upper Paleolithic region of your own humanity. It could send you, bleeding and howling like a werewolf or a wounded jackal into the twisted 70,000 dew-kissed vines and trees and dried riverbeds, into the cool naked terrifying night that looms just beyond Thursday's backyard, just beyond the edge of it, where the hogpin it situated, a proper distance from the chicken coop. The invisible poisoned snakes of this monstrosity could possibly eat the tissues of your cranium—just watching some one shoot a hog brings your own death upon you where your courage is lean.

B.B. says to me, You stand guard. Watch out for Thursday . . .
If you see her coming just whistle.

Okay.

He and Grew lead the mule, a brown patchy scraggly thing,
away, behind the hedge. I try to watch the house, where Thursday sings a spiritual, and the mule rite, too.

B.B. is all muscle and black handsome. He stands on a keg
behind the dumb female animal. B.B. has his stubby peter in
his hand and he's standing on tiptoes, yet he's unable to elevate
himself to the level of the horse's vagina. The dumb animal
casually looks around to see what's going on at her ass-end. She
slaps B.B. in the face with her tail, and the keg turns over and
he hits the ground, rolls down the hill and ends with his backside soaking wet from the guts and feathers from a recent chick-
en-killing. Grew, unlike me, has no time to laugh at this sight.
He's too busy, now, himself on the erected keg, with his erect
penis in his hand, trying to plunge into the animal. Grew is
taller and comes closer to making it, sooner. But not quite. I
watch the big black lips of the overworked, sickly-looking beast
of burden. The pussy lips pucker. And suddenly, Grew drives
his thing in, and begins pumping. Meanwhile, the mule's tail
beats him across the face until he's blind with tears. Yet, Grew
refuses to stop. He obviously means to finish.

I know there's no chance for me to get up there, I'm too little.
If anything, I'd better snatch a hen and go behind the coop.

Grady Flower's wheelchair has a round hole in its seat and his
ass fits over it. Beneath the chair, there's a pot. When he has
to empty his bowels or relieve himself of urine, the pot is al-

64

ways handy. It reduces Thursday's work, also: she has only to remove the pot, empty it, and return it. All the time, Grady's old, old wrinkled rear-end and his organs are suspended over the enamel slopjar; in other words, when he's not in his wheelchair, he's in bed. Life for him has come to this circuit. He's a lean, bony old white man, with white hair, and he looks upon the world from deep, angry faded blue eyes. I'm afraid of him.

> His odor is often overpowering, when I lie on the floor in his room to look at the pictures in his old geography books, trying to imagine what all of those states, countries, and continents were like. Grady, because these were his books, had seen them all. Yet he stank. From beneath his chair comes a *drip drip* sound.

It is late. Thursday is in the dining room, humming and practicing her fine art; ironing other peoples' clothes. For money, of course. Gal is asleep. Somebody's girl is always asleep. Almost anybody is always about to sleep.

> Thursday left us lying on our bellies looking at slick photographs in slick magazines, on the floor in Grady's room. Grady, before the fireplace, the fire burning low, and Grady in his wheelchair, napping.

The look in Grew's eyes says he has an idea. Then, Grew, with his mouth says, I have an idea.

> Okay.

Is it about agriculture? asked B.B.

> No; it's geomantic, Grew said, smartly. Clicking his tongue against his teeth. He continued, softly: Have you guys ever seen the old man's dick—the size?

No, said B.B. I figured one *no* was enough so I didn't say another one. I waited, still wondering what geomancy had to do with anything. (I'm always concerned with what Grew has to say, even when he doesn't know what he's talking about. I like him a fraction better than I like B.B.).

> Come on, said Grew.

Grew started crawling toward Grady's bed. On hands and knees, too, B.B. and I followed. (I was always following but somehow I was never quite *with* them).

This idea is going to be fun, Grew said gleefully.

Standing against the wall at the head of Grady's bed was a broom made of straw from the fields. Grew carefully broke three straws from the broom and with solid care placed one in B.B.'s and one in my hand; keeping the final one, he lowered his shoulders, with the straw, now, in his mouth, and looking back, motioned for us to follow his lead.

> It was dusty and stifling beneath the bed, but worse than that was the rancid odor of Grady's pot beneath his wheelchair, which we could see at the foot of the bed. His chair was close and it was the only thing we could see from under there.

We crawl slowly and as quietly as we can toward the foot. When we can stick our heads from under and look up directly beneath Grady's chair, we situate ourselves. Already trying to assess the unusual situation we see.

> Wow! whispers B.B., who *thought* he himself had the biggest weapon in the world—until now.

I can see Grady's huge sagging triangle of organs but I can't figure out what's hanging on the head of his penis. It really looks like a little cabbage into which his thing has been crammed. Slowly, from all sides of the vegetable—*I'm sure it's a vegetable!*—there is a leakage, drip, drip, drip, into the pot. Weird! really *super*weird

> Poor old man. I remember when Thursday was sick that time, and Nasteylipp was looking after Grady—she used to lock him up in the closet in his room, him sitting in his chair, like that; she'd leave him in there all day, day after day, and would simply throw a piece of cornbread in on his lap once in awhile. I hated the old creep but it still brought tears to my eyes.

Now, Grew ran his piece of straw out, a long curved thing, and began tickling Grady's great droopy balls. While the damn cabbage continued to drip . . . whatever it was discharging. The old man must have V.D. of the spirit, I thought. If not, what did the vegetable mean? Grew's straw wiggled the crevices. I waited breathlessly for Grady to shout. Nothing happened. Grew continued to poke at the old man's appendage. If the coot wasn't going to respond it might be all right for me to take a stab at him, too. I jabbed him in the balls and B.B. began to poke, with his straw, at the cabbage suspended on the end of the head of the long limp organ. I felt that somehow we were committing a very great "sin" and it felt quite good. But reducing my "guilt" was that damn cabbage. It was obviously Grady's secret. And being an old helpless man, naturally he had no right to such a secret. Somebody, probably Thursday, at least, shared it with him. The secret I mean. Or maybe that was the way she soaked her vegetables before cooking them. Maybe Thursday really was a witch! Anyway, the old man, I was beginning to think, had no feeling in his sex organs, cause he was taking the ends of our sharp straws without a flinch.

> That is, until I accidentally jab him too hard. I lost my balance, is what caused it. And he let out a bellow that made the never-used wine glasses in the cupboard in the hall shake against each other, doing a song and dance. I think he said: THURSDAY! COME AND GET THESE BASTARDS BEFORE I KILL 'EM!

Meanwhile we scrambled from under the bed and got back to the magazines spread on the floor before Thursday managed to respond. We were innocently turning the pages when she came into the room.

Thursday's house is situated on a hill that drops into the woods. You can stand up beneath the back porch. The farther you go beneath the house the less space there is between the bottom and the ground. B.B., Grew, and I were under there as far as we could get, and we had a stray cat beneath an upsidedown pot, the big black kind Thursday uses for making lye soap in the back yard.

Talk quietly, B.B. said.

I didn't say anything, I said. I wanted to know how long could the animal be expected to survive without air. But I didn't ask —how would they know . . . ?

Let's kill it, said Grew. There was a gleam in his eye.

We shouldn't kill it, B.B. said.

I said it again, We shouldn't kill it, Grew. Let it live.

Polecats fall in wells and stink up water, said Grew.

But this isn't a polecat, I said. I brushed a splatter of webs from my hair and eyelids.

Maybe we *should* kill him, said B.B., cause he'll be a polecat when we finish with him. Haw haw haw.

Let's not kill it, I said, rather, let's take it up to Dischel's and Papanek's place and dump it in the cage with the man.

There isn't any cage up there, said Grew. They're free and they're white. In fact, he went on, they're pretty nice people: they wouldn't even keep an animal in a cage, let alone a man. Papanek gave me a watermelon once, last summer.

Listen, said B.B., let's do something with this creepy cat before Thursday or Slick John catches us.

Suddenly Grew lifts the huge heavy pot, reaches beneath and by the neck drags the feline creature out. A trail of soft dust behind it. The dust beneath the house is the softest I've ever seen or tasted. Its texture is like luxury, and it's terrible to touch like touching "air." Or nothing or space.

Moses, you go out first, look around. If the coast is clear, signal.

Okay, Grew.

As I leave Grew stuffs the yellow cat into the burlap bag. The cat's yellow eyes are huge glass jewels.

Jewish cat, I said. Then I crawled all the way out.

I brushed the dirt from my overalls and suddenly it started raining. Strange, cause the sky contained no clouds, only sunlight and its everyday unreachable mystery. We had an old well in the backyard that we never used. I often wondered about fresh water that fell into it: rain water getting back down to low rivers so swiftly, while the other drops took days seeping down through the hard, packed earth. I forgot to signal for a moment. Then I remembered. I signaled before I looked to see if we were not being observed. I checked after I signaled and was lucky, as usual. The *coast* was clear.

They came out. The bag in Grew's hand was jumping and saying *meow meow meow meow*. The chickens going *cluck cluck cluck* in the yard heard it and stopped, cocked their jumpy heads, listening.

We go down to the abandoned well.

Grew holds the bag over the opening, the mouth of the well. He looks at each of us. Inside the bag, the cat moves; and he says meow several times again. A crow flies overhead saying *caw caw caw caw caw caw*.

A dog, somewhere, says *raff raff raff!*

Grew turns loose the bag. We hold our breaths. A moment passes. Then, the sound below
SSS-SPLOSH!
And the rain water continues to fall into the well. Everything, in fact, continues as though nothing has happened.

It is a thick early night as we go home along the soft highway. Seems all my life is spent between hard and soft highways. I am disappointed. I am very disappointed. Taking nothing but the ugliest whiff of the glamor home (home?) clutched inside our skulls, like trapped smoke in a coke bottle.

> Before we leave, each of us, except Gal, are allowed to throw a weakly pitched ball at the nigger. That is all we're allowed to do. Nasteylipp giggles. She cocks her arm back, the ball, held lightly in her right hand, goes toward the nigger's head. It misses. With another nickel, she buys another ball.

And again, then says, Shit!

> A gypsy boy, perhaps two years older than I once remember being, squats at the side of a booth where hotdogs are sold, and he pumps his penis. He grins at us as we go by. I wonder why he's not ashamed.

On the outskirts of the circus weird things happen. A grown man is throwing up.

> Nasteylipp licks her lip and douches the air with her restrained laughter. A white man with three kids running around him winks at her. She blushes; imagine her blushing. As we go by, they speak softly to each other.

The wooden horses. They go up and down. As they go around. The underlying principle is simple yet I wonder at the arrangement. Only the white children, the white adults are riding in this circle.

> And the white children; tons of cotton candy and their weightless laughter, in their mouths. Their mothers in cotton dresses. The prints of their panties and their slim, worn legs. The big knotted fists of white men; their flabby jowls.

70

A big Negro, black as warmth, sits on a stool and lets pudgy cackling white men throw horse-turd size balls at him. These men try to knock his head off. Most of the time they miss. Some of the shit some of the time is bound to hit the fan.

Rifles to shoot wooden ducks.

Now that it all has come it looks like a great affair of shocking triteness, like a Negro revival decked with whites. The tents, I mean, the way the pegs go down into the earth, the ropes, how they struggle back from the cloth, holding the canvas stiff at a forty-five degree angle. Like temporary churches.

I'm cold. My nose is running and I hate Lucy Nasteylipp Flower. I also hate B.B. and Grew, now. I hate the spy, Gal.

If I could put a name to each and everything in the circus I might then control it all. Manipulative magic. But will the circus come at night, will it open the daylight or will it come somewhere between day and dark, when certain men threaten to cut off the heads of helpless little children who will never grow up, who are cursed to remain small and defenseless? What colors will the circus become?

She sank her line in and ripples moved around it. Almost instantly, the kicking, the *splash*ing. She jerks the line up and skillfully unhooks the catfish's mouth, deposits it in an oblong straw basket that is lined with newspaper.

Sounds.

Crickets, and other awful, thudding night cries. Things like *coo coo coo* and *hoo hoo hoo*. Or silence and the empty vacuum of the damp tension.

The mud in the road we took was soft and mushy and ran in long streaks. Took off my shoes. Tied the strings together. Carried them around my neck. B.B. and Grew trudged along ahead of me, barefoot and singing, Tenderfoot, tenderfoot, tenderfoot!

The moon was bright. Quite bright.

Catfish bite better at night, she explained.

Wish they hadn't told me about it. Something like that that's coming and never ever gets here. I'd rather simply be shaken

71

awake at midnight and have cold water thrown on my face, told to get into my pants, and come along. Thursday speaking: We're going, she said.

And the long walk along the highway. The pavement is still hot, though its night.

Don't ask questions, Thursday said, and don't wear your *good* shoes.

A car, you could hear one advancing, would go, WOOSH, passing us, like a rocket. She is carrying her fishing pole.

Anyway everything is beside the point. I have to keep doing things to practice patience. Like Tom Mix in the comic books. The fat ass of his horse rides off, away from our eyes. He kicks the horse. That's what I want. But the black people have broken-down horses. The broken-down white couple down the road, who pick their own cotton (too poor to hire niggers, have an upstanding proud stallion who pulls the plow that turns the fresh black earth evenly. When Slick comes to plow Thursday's garden, the old horse he brings drops turds every second and drags along, his miserable head hung very low. I want to ride a great, fine horse. I want one that will gallop off into the sunset like Silver. Or a pinto like Tonto's. Yet, the point is: I shouldn't keep craving and craving. It even hurts the tension pushed against the knowledge of the coming circus.

Yet, as it stood, those posters were the only specific traces. I hadn't heard a truly episcopal word on the morality, whether or not such an event or incident was sinful. Which is most important to know. If (*even* if) you are doing a study. But I shouldn't force you back into yourself so often. It's too fair, too honest. Stay with me.

The thought preoccupied me a long time.

Thursday hadn't said anything one way or two ways. Which is even more important. And I felt my lips shake every time I thought of asking her. How would I phrase it or why should I bother. Like laughter, I figured a circus had to be sinful. Shit, how could a circus *not* be sinful: it was happy! The soft curse of the invisible devil hid in the joy. Like playing, too much playing at ground level was also dangerous and wasteful. One had to keep driving (at something) like a maniac or a dumb, foolhearted lover. Or Christ's blue eyes would move in the picture (follow you) from the wall in the dining room. His girlish fingers pressed upon his red, red heart would tighten if you somehow made a mistake. Pure tribal psychology.

A horsefly stayed vertical one day all day between his eyes. I was glad. Only twitching its wings, rubbing its antennas together. The sonofgod held down by a horsefly. My mind was undergoing a metamorphosis, just observing his cool, his stillness. I wondered if I ran out into the road in front of a coming truck would it kill me. Painstaking thoughts that had no beginnings, no ends.

I automatically began remembering things Moses Westby had told me. Like he was on the trail with that badass Ben Hodges, a notorious cattle thief and gyp artist. The man who once guarded us learned a lot by knocking around with that old badman. They rustled cattle all through the Southwest and westward, to the North, through Nebraska, where he wanted to rewrite all the road signs. Moses also ran around with Hi Hatch and Albert Potter. He was a witness to the great St. Johns, Arizona, fight between those two cats. He could have turned Deadwood Dick in for $500 Reward but Moses was no fink. After all, he and Nat Love, better known as Deadwood Dick, had mutual memories of the Black Hills. That's why I say Moses could've told me anything I wanted to know about the denomination of that particular circus.

If he were here now he could hip me to what the circus will be like. Nobody here now gives a shit about the degrees or the angles of my mind. If Veronica was here perhaps she'd care. Grady is too sick. Thursday is too religious, too mean. Slick has no tongue, only fists. Nasteylipp, the whore, has eyes that are too narrow, too red, and lips that are too dry to speak of the future contents, of a circus. Moses, only Moses Westby would take the time to voice it. He'd show me the thing in microcosm. You've never heard him tell stories, have you?

His stories are always true. That is why they sound so funny and sometimes like lies. Y'know what I mean?

Whether or not Veronica approved anything Moses was a good scientist. Always had his misplaced talents somewhere in store.

A cold storage. Nobody, outside me, understood what a genius Moses Westby really was.

Belonging to the sex that begets babies by fertilizing the egg. How Veronica used Moses, how she used me. Yet, I must have been seasick a long time waiting for the stark-looking legal possessors of the helpless flesh and the unbound spirit. Moses came in low like an insecticide sprayer two-engine plane doing the watusi over a Georgia cotton field. Yes, about that low, close, but careful. Some bird, Thursday told us, that was how we all came. Not knowing that Moses had already shown me his dirty pictures, showing how lovely six people could make sex together, teasing life. Now this is called a blowjob now this is called screwing a broad now this is called homosexuality just so when you start school no little dumb kid will mislead ya.

> I refuse to think about the circus cause it's taking too damn long to come to town. Maybe it's a joke, maybe the confusion and the posters and the allusions are all designs, evil whiffs. Maybe I won't be able even to lead up to it, let alone walk away. Maybe I'll have to actually create it, make it stick, before it's really convincing. But I shouldn't have to do it that way: it should be *in* me like it was once there, beside the dusty road that leads through town; posters about it on every telephone-light pole.

No, around the edge of town. On the outskirts of Lynch-burg County, way back from Chickamauga, far from the farm-house on highway 69, beyond Remus Road, past Sodacracker Heights, all the restricted areas, the Rehabilitation Center, the other impressive sites. A circus would always choose the outer limits of a penal area or town. And that must be the reason we first and finally went through town. We knew the danger of drunk white men who might have wanted to use us for sport. White men, it is said, are great lovers of sport. Moses once said that and he also said they get their rocks from a bloated love of horseplay. I've seen people die from simple horseplay.

I don't mind giving even my hands to things. I would give my feet to more than paths, streets, highways. I always end up or begin on highways. I'd give *myself* to more than the simple chill of water if the understanding that I cannot swim was taken seriously. I'm on loan here. I'm the spoils of warfare, temporarily locked up, but stealing more and more tender moments of true freedom, and thus liberating the world.

Even to *invent* a circus, I think, I suspect, is painful. The futility of it, y'know. Words. Your pleasure, my obsession. All this time, I've been talking about the distance between grown people and children.

Then, there are ditches. I like jumping, or trying to jump to the other side of a ditch. It's an engagement that is malicious. I admit that it is also a bit *much* for me, at any age, though I remain always ageless. Or I am either very young or very old. Something incongruous about this. Yet the ditch in the pasture on the outer limits of the town has to be crossed. Maybe we go through a cow pasture but what about those horses fucking the other day? I've made it across twice so far, two times out of two hundred attempts.

I want to stop referring to myself as "I," but when the chance comes it has to be effective, very special; or I must forget it: no matter how sick I am of "I."

You know ditches can be found alongside highways. If I have to hide in a ditch at any given moment, I'll let you know.

Anyway, you might see horses screwing on this route. And that *is* amazing to see. A stallion pouncing at a sixty-degree angle upon the she-animal. Like a peninsula breaking, crashing into the belly of a continent.

We don't really have to come back through town. Especially since we don't like doing it. And it isn't necessary to look at the posters again. The white faces scare me anyway. They are not nice. We walk across the white and red dirt, through the pasture; the short cut, home.

All the time spent in the one-room schoolhouse was busy. I drove a red truck up and down the bench. I was waiting. Finally, Grew gave me a tiny part of what to expect: a circus, he said, is where you eat cotton candy and candy apples and ride plastic horses around and around.

Free people walk through town eating ice cream cones. Some of the mean-looking ones smoke cigars. They are all, in any case, very frightening: their distance. One, one day said to me, while you are black, while I am white, I hate you, I hate my-self.

I envy their happiness, I pity their pointless freedom. But the people close to me, I hate passionately. One day I may have the courage to kill them, all.

Yet these distant ones, may they discover acid at the bottom of their cones. Or may they discover themselves. Or may their roots shrink from the poison at their core.

There are posters first. On the way to school, when we go through town. Or we go through town deliberately just to see the slant, to read the bold bright red words.

BARNUM & BAILEY CIRCUS

Simply the idea of a circus, it did not mean: to do evil. It would have been too synthetic an idea but it was less brutal than everyday life. Something special suddenly has come and it applies, no matter how remotely, to me.

2
the
witch
burning

Then abruptly we had come to face it: a wide gaping mouth of green growth. Thousands of Indian bodies packed into it. The sides were studded with stunted trees and the bottom, what you could actually see of it, was jagged with weeping branches of rare trees and spruce and splendor of one natural kind or another. It was the most stunning crevice I'd ever seen, even more captivating than Gal's cunt, or the sap holes in trees into which I sometimes tried to pry. Who had the gods done it to to produce all this magic? The bodies were a natural part of it and didn't detract or shock. Sharp spires snapped up from its depths, but nothing down there stood very high, and right now, in the middle of summer, the water-oriented earth, at the floor, was invisible, even where the bodies didn't cover it, so that, if we were going to see skulls from long ago we'd have to somehow get down there, and there was no visible way to scale the wall down and certainly no way at all to get out once down. And ancient dead skulls weren't worth that much; so, anchored under massive fear and wonder, awed, we turned back and started back.

Meiosis, said B.B.

What is a melanin? said Grew.

I didn't say that. Just watch out. That birch.

We went beneath its satin, a stringy eucalyptus snapped toward our skulls. Gal was whimpering and complaining to Thursday about her blooming bruised goosefeet.

Be careful now, said Thursday.

Because of the Indian arrow heads? said B.B.

No. Any minute now you're going to step right up to the edge of the canyon and if you're not careful you'll end up dead, in hell, at the bottom of it. The edge is very steep. Old Mister Hallet, years ago, fell. Died instantly.

The graveyard was always across the highway from the house. And it was always night even when the sun pretended to make time day. We were gathered "factors" in a 16th-century nightmare. (The people around the "I" were strangers. The "I," too, was a stranger to himself, and to the others. I cannot honestly say I believe I am a great sage and lawgiver. That I wrote five books and transformed my people into a god-fearing nation with social order and stern discipline. But if I came out of the river, so did all people.) I loved the trees more than the people and I felt like a racketeer's son, locked in a boarding school. A segmented and ritualistic penal life, with exposure to the graveyard out front, and the dense hilly thicket below the back yard. Nice life for a strange shepherd with a Mosaic touch of madness, wouldn't y'say? But I'd already begun dreaming of a prison break; though not yet did my daydreams dwell on such a possibility.   The strangeness of the trees, their way of breathing, their roots, how they clung to the earth or brushed each other, but mainly the hard core of their simple presence, which involves so much that is untouchable—their design, their conduct, their effect—is what got swiftly to me. And not only the trees. The bushes, the grass, the smell of rocks and damp earth, the crumbling of yellow, black, red, white earth in the palm of my hands, and how it tastes. The huge wonder of it all! The leaves, dried or still green, the evergreen needles beneath my naked foot, the cones, the twigs, the fragrance of the bark, the sap and especially the sweet overpowering taste and odor of honeysuckle! The Dogwood blossoms! I ate any and everything I could find and survived poison ivy only by some miracle. (Once Grew got trapped in the stuff and broke out, sores spreading up his arms and wherever he scratched, to his neck and face, around his mouth, up his legs and thighs, standing deep in the juice of its weed.) Ah! but Laurel Oak pushing its mighty sharpness over and through us, near the blackberry vines, might cure even blight of the soul! I like to say such things, anyway. I liked, too, hanging out at the edge of the fig tree, the one with an inscription left by a Big Hammock. That was before the settlement of the Seminole. The markings still baffle me. Things like: New Deal, NATO, "Electoral College," "do not beg like a Oglala Sioux," and stranger than that, "Apache wart." I didn't lose any sleep over any of 'em. Thursday, because of her Indian "blood," pretended to understand and explain it all to us, once. Anyway, she had gone with us that first day we saw the canyon of death where the Indians, her ancestors, used to commit suicide. She couldn't tell me any more than my eyes could see. Maybe the others believed her. I only pretended to.

> Thursday had talked about the canyon for years but she hadn't actually taken a look at it since the day Old Mister Hallet fell in.

As a girl and as a young woman Thursday had turned her lust toward the city, or the big town. Even while giving a simple lesson in geography, she remained a distinctly terrifying creature—a tall, gaunt, black woman with hair pulled tightly back into a hard, black- and gray-streaked knot, who moved along, under the crisp brown mulberry, magnolias, pine, laurel oak, the leaves cracking, snapping, beneath her black, stringup high-top shoes, clad in a deep-purple cotton dress which had a simple white ruffle around her deep blue neck. But the dress hung loosely from her shoulders. And she was always whispering or humming or talking to herself. Mostly though, like a bird, she was singing. When she thought about the Indian side of her family, her ancestors, she would whine, sometimes out loud, the word, *genocide*. She could say it distinctly, slow: gen-o-cide.

> We followed a path to the canyon almost completely covered beneath years of turns and accidents of nature. When this area was once the bottom of the sea. And it is still the bottom of something.

We had a little instrument with a "hand" that constantly pointed north. I held it in my hand as we walked. It made you wonder about the fundamental problem of anthropogenesis, if you had the nerve. Or just simple human achievement.

What if we took a wrong turn, lost the true path, following (though walking in front of) Thursday? Would she be able to say, with a sturdy nod of her Mohegan-head, This way, not that way? Thursday, in any case, was wise about certain things. She had a good nose and hawk eyes. And a memory. She remembered Gabriel's, Nat Turner's, Denmark Vesey's and Quaco's great slave revolts; and, as a child she had herself with her Indian mother slaved with 333 Africans and 233 Indians in Rhode Island. Thursday always told us it was cause of TV that slavery finally came to an end. She might have something there, I think.

Once in awhile I'd glance back and catch the lines throbbing in Gal's face. Obviously she'd have been happier in the city where we came from, in Moses' restaurant, digging in the ice-cream pits. This physiography was definitely not her speed. Anyway, it was while we were moving along in a line like Alaskan scouts that Thursday stopped and applied the dull purple-edged dwellings nesting in her eyesockets to the ancient carvings left by her folks.

> Death was a custom, Thursday said. She said it softly. Like talking to herself.

I was dying to see the bottom of it. Knowing that it'd be stacked with a mosaic range of twisted broken brittle bodies. Bones and skulls. Teeth.

> We beat back undergrowth. Ahead of me, Grew and B.B., just being ahead of me, were rubbing me the wrong way. I felt I should be leading!

The roar was nearer. The cars were coming around again. Closer. How many times did the game require they go around? They were headed around once more. Then it happened.

It was car Number 26, driven by Jack Ashbrook. He was only a few yards from our bewitched eyes, and through the cloud of dust I saw his face die. His eyes were swollen, and his teeth clinched. His fingers grasping the steering wheel. The helmet was fitted tightly down over his pink skull. The blue collar of his jacket. The yellow paint of his outer metal. It was so "instant" you saw it after it happened.

The car swerved, the wheels turned too quickly. I'd done it many times with my trucks, wrecked them. A frontal problem. Dissonance. Over and over Number 26 went and everybody (except a woman in labor about to have a baby right in the front row) screamed, started running down the inside. To get a closer look, see. Moses Westby didn't move, so I didn't move. I looked up at his face, and he was busy lighting a fresh cigarette. Calmly, his good eyes squinted behind his dark sunglasses. Meanwhile, Gal was swooning and when she wasn't swooning she was yaking. Creolized language, trade language, contact vernacular, *our* thing.

WOOOOOOOOOOOOO WOOOOOOOOOOOOOOOOOOOOO WOOOOOOOOOOOOO

GOOD GOD HAVE MERCY

JESUS LOOK AT HIS HEAD

THE BLOOD IN HIS EYE

EEEEEEEEEEEEEEEEEEEEEEEEEEEEEEEEEEEEE! (The pregnant woman delivers while seeing death.)

Through the clearing as the other race cars continued around the track I saw Number 26 drenched in flames. And resting on its side. The side of the car, yellow, faced the sky, also yellow. Ladies were still screaming. Exclamation pitch! A Negro woman with a paper hat on her head, one wearing her boyfriend's cloth cap, was silent, in shock. *His face,* said her boy friend, did you see his face?

The woman had covered her eyes.

His face was full of blood behind the glass, and he was trying to open the door but he couldn't, said the boyfriend. He looked like he might have been a trustee, somewhere. That kinda goodness oozing from him.

And the other cars were still swimming and blasting through the heat. The blue flames stroked the skyline.

The day reached the fullness nature plotted for it. A lemon looming in the sky, too bright for words. The cars were all shabby, ugly, painted, though; and the colors were big, bold, sorta nice, childish colors, primary, holy mary. Like red, blue, yellow. They rattled and banged, even sitting still. This sort of action, simple things, I can handle, like death is quite simple, primary. Echo word.

The dust from the ground moved slowly up through the space, behind the impact of footfalls. If the edge, the limb of a narrow tree moved somewhere near, it was unnoticed. If somebody in the forest whistled nobody heard him.

The gypsies somewhere in the huge background didn't (with luck) share this anxiety-ridden moment of sensuality and death. Through the loudspeaker the voice sounded hoarse: ON YOUR MARK—The motors coughing (all the drivers were white, twenty-one, free, and American). The drivers climbed into the cabs of their machines. Number 26 was first. (Like a soldier stepping out down onto a land mine.) Trying to look movie-star cool, casual, hip. An elastic moment of joy. The final accent of possible victory. They had fixed-stress. A long slack purple ribbon hung across the track. Each car had parked its nose near it. I kept watching Moses' eyes, but his face told me only that something was about to end. Except the day and the glossy black and white faces all around said something different, spoke of a beginning. But Moses was always different. GET SET— the voice commanded.

Moses Westby's lips quivered. They were dry. His Adam's apple moved like a slow fan across the face of a Christian in a Georgia church. Slow as a Chattanooga frog jumping from a sandstone into a hot puddle.

Moses stuck the end of his cigarette into his mouth. As he sucked in his jaws I watched his eyes narrow behind the beautiful glasses he wore. I really envied him as much as I loved him. If only I could be so smooth! So masculine, a *first* person! Moses had an acute accent, but I couldn't quite place it, yet I always tried to imitate it. Now that he'd come back to visit us I felt contaminated, corrupted by his presence—the force of his life, so close. His bright sport shirt looked so peaceful, so glad to be next to his skin. READY—

Then, I noticed that Gal was holding Moses' hand. There was no hand for me to hold. The cigarette was using it. I reached up and scraped the silky side of his body. His strong smoke drenched my senses until my eyes watered, until I felt sick with loneliness and jealousy and even physical pain. and, GO—

The crowd gave a sudden though not strange blast. A kinda insane, existential moment, it made sense, dimly. To me. If I could just "let go" and feel such an explosion I too might on that day no longer commit the dream of lonely Capricorn in search of Cancer, Cancer would (or could) become a girl, to love; *who knows!* it could be that such an incident would also free me of my longing for Veronica. I may stop falsely searching for a "security" that never did nor ever will exist. Moses, too, in my mind, might take his proper place. Yes, his *proper* place. To just simply burst *out*—like that!

The rickety fence shook from the force of their excitement. Man, *did* they move out! In the crowd, at the most intense moment, I caught sight of Slick. *What was he doing here?* At his side, jumping and screaming, was a chocolate woman, not Lucy N. The new woman, however, looked very much like Nasteylipp. People move in circles. I move in big circles. Ripples. I noticed, in this new place, that Slick looked gently

85

crushed in the chemistry of some odd crucible. This feeling, despite his own and the face next to his, against which he, dark purple, sunswept (rare for a moonlight man) took rest in the tension of playtime laughter. Was it social guilt? It was somewhat like seeing Slick in a happy dream in which he had no right to penetrate.

The sight of Slick's face took me from a segment of the race and I instantly increased my hatred for him the moment I realized the loss. The gutty buzzing, the dust now in my nose, the shouts, all of this, but mainly the speeding colorful metal things out there going around in an inside circle, and the feeling of Moses' arm near my own, made up the world I wanted to make peace with.

It may sound irrational but the thought crossed my mind: what would Slick do to me if he saw me. Could (or would) Moses protect me from Slick's violence? I couldn't remember whether it was in a dream or Slick had actually spoken the words: I'm gonna cut off your ear as soon as I get a sharp knife!

That moment passed. Though Slick's strangely happy and eminent face still loomed there, on the other side of other faces. I looked out and couldn't see the cars now moving in a scramble of dust way away. Why?

And the loudspeaker: Number 26, Jack Ashbrook, on the outside; third place, Sam Litton, Number 22; second place, Bob Shufflebot, still in the lead; he's Number 33; but Tony Welsh, Number 84, moving up from fourth place now—he's nose to nose with Ashbrook, and . . .

Moses mashed out his cigarette. I watched the glossy toe of his shoe spin in a half arc, first this then that way; the threads of his shoe, I loved the neat, expensive threads. The gloss. The smell of his leather. They must have cost a thousand dollars, those shoes. When his toe finished with the cigarette, neatly it was lifted, moved slowly back to the spot where it had stood previously. I was amazed at his precision. One day, I want to be that good at what I do.

What ever you do, one fine day you do it no more. Jack Ashbrook was a name, there were numbers attached to him. If there was music for him in the air, it now ended. It may have come at a moment of glory—he was passing Tony Welsh.

Moses?

Whenever someone called that Biblical name I always thought surely they must be addressing Moses Westby, the guard, not Moses Westby, the inspector. This tendency, then, explains why I didn't bother to answer when Moses spoke to me.

Moses had just parked the car in marshy terrain.

We were early for the stock-car race. Just before it snapped off the motor of Moses' Cadillac sounded like some animal trying to vomit. It was so hot the odor of the seat covers hung heavy in my senses. Gas fumes, too, drenched me. Somebody was racing a motor a few cars down in the parking lot. The outer skin of Moses' face fascinated me. His dark eyes were dancing behind his dark glasses.

I pull up the button. The door opens under the prediction of my knotted fingers. My feet touch the wet black earth. I look down at the patches of soggy dark-green grass. I feel very happy. I pull up a handfull, I chew it slowly. Ah! overhead, the ancient trees offer an umbrella from the baking sun. I fill my lungs full of air; exhaling, I also spit out the stems, leaves, and flower spikelets. I look up through the trees: overhead, high in the clouds, a tiny man floats along in a cab suspended from a huge bright-pink and bright-green baloon.

Anyhow, the people move toward a specific circle.

Only a moment ago we'd driven into this town from the highway. Coming from Thursday's farmhouse on highway 69, we came through America, its United States, along controlled highways, interchanges, toll highways, seeing signs *jump* at us, like INTERSTATE, DRIVE CAREFULLY, GO SLOW, SPEED LIMIT: 65 MILES PER HR., advertisements for toilet tissue, Coca-Cola, beer, and motels; I knew I'd never forget the dull names of the places we swept through in the Cadillac. Places like Albany, Hutchinson, Moose Lake, Northfield, Silver Bay, Willmar, Big Falls, Danbury, New Bedford, Dedham, and Clinton. When I was on the road either before or after this particular trip I realized that all the states in North America contained cities and towns with endless duplicate names. Ugly,

ugly! Though now I had a partial index map I still couldn't locate the name of the town in which we now found ourselves witnessing people (including ourselves) about to go goggle-eyed at a race and a death. Coming down the steep hill into this town, however, was quite an experience. Circling slowly, the heavy Cadillac took the road with ease. We moved downhill through the paddy neighborhood. It was composed of rich, well-kept houses with green American lawns and white American picket fences. The façade of smug, puritanical wasps. I began to lose the suspicion that we were necessarily in the South.

This is a lynch town, if there ever was one, said Moses.

What is a lynch town, Moses? asked Gal.

A place where fragile connoisseurs of joy reside in the comfort of one another's rationalization. (The Cadillac now reached the bottom and began to creep along the leveled road.) I could see that the town down there, now before us, as we entered it, to reach the other side where the race track was, generated a quiet, tribal intensity as it swam up visually into my eye with the dullness of a trading stamp from some dense supermarket of outlaw landscape bespeaking Victorian prudery. But passing through the black ghetto was very much like tripping through a Mississippi Prison Farm, the hovels, the mean, wretched huts, the sheds, all, blunt and real, yet symbolic. Yeah. Slavery was a national concept and freedom, a sectional consideration.

Now, we went strolling toward the gates with the others.

Moses stepped gently just to be sure he didn't violate some fucked-up taboo. He was looking around. He was using his heart, and he was using his instincts and his fingertips. He could smell his direction. Penal wisdom. For instance, if he went through the gate marked "white" he could be penalized, lose credits, almost anything could happen. His senses therefore were very sharp and we too were automatically picking it up. I had already learned how *pretty* some white folks can be. They could be pretty dreadful. Moses was as careful as a bird building a nest. For some reason I can't fully fathom I now remembered sharply that blind construction worker I once heard trapped inside his unpainted hut; he'd built it the wrong way, and was then trying to kick down the walls.

Looks like rain, said Moses.

We were standing in line but the line was going no place.

We're early, said Moses. Let's go sit under a tree.

So, we did.

Well, said Gal, smoothing out her print dress, *I* hope it doesn't rain.

The arrangement of lines in Moses' face laugh. We're insulated beneath the limbs of a tree, a big one. I look away from him. I take from my back pocket my red firetruck and begin racing it along my thigh and leg, making sounds for it. Sometimes you'd think I was a senile old man. But I enjoy playing with firetrucks. They remind me of fires. And flames throw off excitement.

Suddenly, while moving the truck I said, One day I want to marry a woman like Veronica.

Veronica is white, said Moses.

Veronica, said Gal to Moses, is just Veronica.

Moses chuckled. He looked at me. *Why?*

Why—what?

Why should you ever want *to marry,* huh?

I don't know, I said.

Let's walk around, Moses said, standing up, brushing off the seat of his pants. He straightened his necktie. He coughed a sudden smokers' cough, as he took the lead.

The wet earth puckers beneath our footfalls. Put three "related" people together on a sick landscape, slide the magnetic force they each ooze, then locate (if you can) their center of gravity. My toe kicked a brass washer.

A girl, dark, like us, sifting something, squatting in tall grass by a river. Long, silky black hair. Chickasaw, Cherokee?

No, said Moses Westby. Gypsy.

Is there an indictment against them, too?

Yes.

What is a Gypsy? said Gal.

An idea.

We strolled on.

Gypsies travel, I said, feeling very bright. Behind such a comment.

I travel, too, said Moses; does that make me a Gypsy?

Does it?

At the end of the clearing there is a trailer attached to a two-door Ford painted dark green.

We began walking along the edge of the river.

When I travel again, I said, I want to go to India, Afghanistan, Greece, Albania, and Bulgaria.

Why?

Because I've never been to those places.

Walking along, I notice an Indian symbol carved into a tree. A yellow toy balloon floats on the water, downstream. Near the edge of the water are stones of white onyx and garnet and moonstone. A bird somewhere overhead in a tree whistles.

I look back. The Gypsy girl has a piece of wire and she's dipping it down into the water, now. She brings it up, soggy weeds clinging to its end. She slams it down into the water. *Plosh!* In the distance, the roar of motors.

Are we missing the race? asked Gal.

No, said Moses. They are simply getting ready.

At that moment a Gypsy (male) about as old or nearly as young as I am, made himself visible. Obviously conscious of our presence. Flaunting himself.

With a sturdy stride of arrogance he walked directly up to me. Snatched the red firetruck from my hand. And the Gypsy ran. He ran across the river, dragging himself out on the other bank with three fourths of his trousers wet. He looked back, thumbed his nose at me and I laughed. Wonderful! Beautiful!

I looked at Moses, who seemed upset. What's the matter?

Don't worry, said Moses, rubbing my head.

I'm not worried.

The three of us held hands.

In front of the trailer we stopped.

Moses called out. *Hello! Anybody there?*

For some unknown reason the date came to my mind. I couldn't do anything with it. But it made itself present, it was September 5th. I felt no anger, no frustration, no hard-shelled pain. I was in check.

Moses was about to bellow again when a happy cylinder-shaped face, dark, containing a heavy, handlebar mustache, stuck itself out the doorway, and glowed, smiling, down into our own. In his "strange" tongue we were offered an unmistakably warm greeting. Pleasantly, Moses rocked back and forth on his heels. He explained, in his only language—English—what had happened concerning the red firetruck. Judging from the expressions passing across this Gypsy's face, he not only understood Moses' language but also took the incident described quite seriously. He was frowning and casting his eyes about in search of the other Gypsy.

The Gypsy's dark face clouded and deepened with blood. Beneath its texture. His large, dark eyes, like mystic searchlights for daylight. To save time. To cover space. His chest swelled. His voice boomed and the sounds amounted to the other Gypsy's name. Some name like Walpurgis.

Instantly the one called came around from the opposite side of the trailer. He held out his hands so that we all could witness his innocence.

See, he said.

But the Gypsy in the doorway had not yet become unserious-looking. He was also obviously suspicious. But it didn't really matter to me.

Go get it, said the Gypsy from the doorway, wherever you hid it, and return it, *instantly!*

The "thief" Gypsy, who, I now noticed, had beautiful golden skin and large dark eyes, looked offended by the command. He drew his lips in to a tight, small line. His nose quivered. Then, he turned and ran away, around the trailer. Where he had stood, the ground became wet.

The man in the doorway tried to smile again but this time it was obviously a bit difficult for him.

The Gypsy "thief" came back and quickly pressed a Carnation flower in my hand. I, just as quickly, dropped it into my pocket, and smiled at him. He returned the smile.

Moses and the other Gypsy now seemed on even better terms.

Gal had been singing to herself and dancing around in a circle.

Nobody now was displeased.

I noticed, as we walked away, that the girl who'd been playing with the piece of wire was now peeping at us from the corner of the metal house (without an address). And I fell in love with her large African eyes, like roses at midnight.

Moses Westby kept his word: he came. His Cadillac looked like the gauge for exhilaration itself as it approached the house. Nobody except possibly Casey Jones drove like that! He drove like a man with guts *and* consideration for the grooves in his tires. Like one hipped to real revelations. He had respect for The Day. In the driveway, he parked the metal monster. It stood there, dripping grease. Something was wrong? The white sand, stained yellow-green. I kept my eye on it. I always watched important things.

Early people, we were. We had been up for hours. Up and down for centuries. Like some one standing out somewhere halfway in the region of accidental altitudes, I felt ageless, seeing Moses again. I never was aware of seeing myself in him. It was a proposition that never entered my mind. I was *already* Moses Westby, despite my other names. Anyhow, it was good to see him and he'd come to keep his word.

My desperation to see a stock-car race was possibly like that of a medieval monk waiting to talk to (his) god. All morning this Saturday I'd waited for him, watching the sun come up over the graveyard. The sun came up like a frightful pigmented face at harvest, coming up out of weeds. For hours I simply couldn't conceive of him *keeping* his word. After all, I believed in nobody except Moses, and only thinly in Moses. The car still dripped hot, black grease. Interesting. The engine, beneath the hood, steaming, hot. Meteoric iron dripping its blood, Moses' communal life-fluid?

> I ran out to meet Moses. I touched the backs of his hands. I kissed his arm. But his eyes were upon Gal, standing on the porch, with a finger in her mouth. In her other hand, behind her back, she was holding the dead bird in which Grew's penis had been kept. As we approached, she calmly dropped it.

Moses stands at the edge of the porch. Gal jumps off into his arms. Her arms around his neck. A tight, tight hug. A hug that spoke of loneliness and love and everything below the level of consciousness. Below speech and outside the scope of memory. I was jealous. He walked to the steps with her in his arms. He climbed the steps and I walked at his side, holding to a tiny area of his pants near the pocket. It was at least a small comfort. I loved him too much, I think.

> I decided not to go into the house with them. I went back to the car. It was an extension of him and through it I could *feel* close to him.

At the wheel, I sat as still as the most ancient implement, the hammerstone. My mind, in it I was the driver. My *value* by some private scale, went *up*. By inches and generations of space/time. Sitting there, I was splitting open the highway, driving so fucking fast! My authority leaving piles of smoke behind me, in the white sky. I was leaving gas fumes of death in dinky kitchens along the unholy road. Even waking up the dead in the graveyard. And all the while, I could hear Moses; his laughter, from the house, was fat. Like his stomach and like some white image of Santa Claus. I remembered how Gal and I once sat on his knees, touching the stubble on his chin. How he'd told us jokes for hours. How he'd kidded us. The plastic, leather seat *smelled*. The ashtray stank. I watched, carefully, the dead bugs smashed against the dirty windshield. A pleasant thought: I was glad he hadn't brought anybody with him. I had dreamed he'd come, bringing a car full of rigid chicks stacked up in pairs like deck queens from some private Hawaiki terrain in a queer homeland, in the city where I came from. Whores softly chewing chewing gum and smelling cheaply of unclean pussy and dime-store perfume. Fat, thick rumps. Tight skirts and powder an inch thick. Wigs that wiggle, fall off. Thick, ruby lips. Or some white or white-looking chick. *No.* Maybe since Veronica he'd given up on white chicks. I saw them coming with him, strungout on some lusty, rude narcotic; all of them out-to-get Moses, to become as intrinsic to him as white is to zinc. Sounding as strange as lovers from a bench in a Russian Orthodox Church in America. And if they *had* come, Thursday would've *blown* their minds, baby! because Thursday could scare anybody "shitless": she was "religious," stern and predictable; *very* predictable! She herself had in her young days been a "cheap bitch," according to Grady (who should know). But Thursday then and Thursday now *couldn't stand* strumpets! and to have one cross her threshold now would be like being vested with the cloud hat, the headgear of the Spanish Inquisition, the black magic spirit! Anyway, my dream was only a dream. Things I was into before falling asleep. And Moses had come alone and I might now succeed in climbing through this strange, potential day. Terms? What are decent terms anyway? If I could keep my ass attached to the same entity where my soul hungout, cool.

Her hand still up, at the edge of the highway, standing, waving. Through the back window of the Cadillac she got smaller, smaller, until I couldn't see her. And that was good. Goodbye, Thursday! If only I could remember her that way forever, with the yardbroom resting against her arm. B.B. and Grew, standing to her side, also waving goodbye. Skinny dark poles moving in the ruptured sunblast. Oh, it felt inexpressibly delightful to be zooming away, to a race! But just *away in*itself was great!

> *Straightahead!* now, the open road, it opens, expands, narrows; all my life, these roads. One of the first things I remember: a road on a rainy night; and Moses' many names and not knowing my own name. Many things, though, I've forgotten. But you know about the rooms, and the piss. And hants at dusk.

We moved along a long time.

Soon, it *was* dark. Night highway under the blast of rain. The white line, in the middle, constantly *coming at me;* into me. Everything we do and say on the way will be worth the race. There are always prices, even under "socialism." Gal is in the middle. I'm near the door. *They are touching each other,* even as he drives.

We still move along a long time.

Rubber against tar. Suddenly we move into daylight. The day is too much.   Flake-white daylight. How happy this moment! Be careful, the door. It might suddenly come open   you resting against it like that . . .

Can you *imagine* it? The countryside, coming alive?

The melody of the rubber against the tar. Hot speed. Inside the lining of *my* happiness there *is* promise. Pure electrum; and my skull throbs, my fingernails against my own skin, from happiness, become savage things! I AM FILLED WITH JOY!!!!!!!

Dig into the eyeballs of this moment—open all inroads! *full speed ahead*

Returning from the race track, we stopped in a town where Moses knew people. The house in which his friends lived was situated deep in the mud on bricks at the far end of a dead-end road. The place boasted no paint, and the early evening sunlight spanked its tin-covered roof. I felt both fear and excitement: it was good to be moving about, seeing new faces, hearing strange new voices, smelling and touching new people.

As we approached, the roof glowed like polished glass at a sixty-degree angle to the sun. The Cadillac, creeping carefully over the deep mudholes, a careful car. The slow, uncommitted slush of the shit along the sides. The radio said, Congress should inspect the President's feces each day just to make sure he ain't eating important secret documents.

Changes, everywhere changes.

Inside the house on the turntable was a disc making music. An early-rock singer was laying on, "Saturday Night Fish Fry," and the sweet, tangy smell of frying fish rolled in torrents from the kitchen, as Moses and Moses(me) and Gal entered. There was gut laughter, too. It also came from the kitchen. Nervously, I crammed my hands down into my pockets. Felt the crushed Carnation, and almost smiled.

Big Mama! Moses called from the front room where we stood, almost uncertain, excluded.

A huge black woman, in a faded flower-print dress, came out with a wide, truly joyous grin etched deep in her face. It was there like it never left. She wore a hairnet over her hair and in her hand she held a long silver fork with a black handle. It took her a moment of squinting before she recognized Moses Westby, but when she did she gave out a massive holler: GOD-DAMN YOU MOSES WESTBY COME HERE AND KISS YO BIG MAMA!!! And he did. They hugged a moment and then she threw her arms around Gal and me and dragged us both against her huge titties, while smacking kisses all over our faces. I didn't know her and I wondered why she liked me. A little disconcerting but nice and I began liking her pretty quickly. Her lips were greasy from Bar-B-Q sauce, I think. But I know she smelled more of armpits than anything else, yet it was not offensive. The odor wasn't deep and stinging, it was mild and almost sweet.

A man and a woman sat quietly on the piano stool, eating fried fish; another couple sat close on the couch discussing the Resurrection of the Dead, the Resurrection of Jesus, David and Bathsheba, and the prophecy of the Antichrist or Gog.

Moses was walking through the house like a nervous tiger and he sipped bourbon from a water glass. Gal had fallen asleep on the couch, her legs curled up, the dirty seat of her drawers exposed to all. That was all right, though it was a good thing Thursday wasn't here. She'd have beat Gal to death

96

in her sleep and made everybody put on a blindfold.　A lot of the people were getting drunk. Some of the men were getting frisky. One reached under a woman's dress and stroked her cunt which made her giggle and playfully slap him.

> Big Mama finished in the kitchen. She took me on her lap in the living room. She was warm and meaty and she whispered love into my ear. She drunkly told me of her private dreams. Things she'd never dared whisper to another ever before. I went to sleep, my face sunk between her tits; her hand, inserted in my pants, resting gently on my quiet flesh.

The eyelids of my mind were heavy. We were driving through a storm, headed back. I dreaded going back. I hated all of them, even Moses now—especially since he was going to keep Gal with him and leave me at Thursday's. We could hardly see the highway, its white line, through the windshield. And Moses was very drunk. The car was zigzagging all over the road. Night seemed an elusive twenty-four inches ahead of us, each inch our vehicle advanced into its (night's) womb. Seldom other cars approached and passed. Mostly, upahead was the endless cloud of gray nothingness—that was the road like a strip of smoke left in the sky by a skywriting airplane. The windshield wipers were sluggish, but doing their best. To the side, dimly, I saw a huge building. Over it, neon red lights flickered: HUMAN RELATIONS CENTER. And the Cadillac continued to swerve dangerously.

> If we die tonight, said Moses, we die *together*. Right?

Right! I said.

> Yeah, said Gal, but Moses, you'd better slow down. You're drunk, y'know.

He knows how to drive.

> *I know* he knows.

Moses laughed. His whiskey breath filled the interior that was already luke warm with our own body odor.

> Moses, said Moses; *you* ain't scared of dying?

Not if I'm with you.

That's the spirit. We die together!

Gal said, Well, I don't especially want to die.

Is Veronica scared of death?

No, Moses, she's not. (Thus spoke my hero). Sometimes, he continued, I think she's already dead.

Moses, said Gal, you're not driving *right*.

What difference does it make, dum-dum? I said.

> At that moment the Cadillac leaned like crazy into a turn as we went around a mountain. It was a narrow, dangerous road. All the road signs pointed this out. KEEP TO RIGHT. GO SLOW. DANGEROUS CURVE. But Moses went right on, at full speed. His rhythm, unbroken. We couldn't see.

But we made it around the mountain and immediately began to drop. The car went into a slide, around and around, and my head was spinning. Darkness, specks of light. The grinding, scraping of the tires against the concrete. Downhill sensation. Gal was screaming. Moses struggled desperately at the wheel. I felt only a slight touch of anxiety—for Moses. At the foot of the hill the Cadillac stopped spinning and simply rolled over into a ditch, nose down. And we sat there, *un*injured; our faces, flat against the front-view window. After a quiet moment of looking sharply at each other the three of us burst out into a beautiful fit of laughter.

I kept falling forward or simply stumbling. But finally I got back to the church and sat on the front steps in its terrible light. The experience had been like a nightmare.

Thursday and other members of the church, inside were chopping away on a song.

Who built the ark?

They screamed.

Ol' Noah built that ark!
Some say Noah was a fool,
But we say he's a wise ol' man!

And they explained why.

For he built his ark on hard ol' ground.
He built that ark outa groper wood!
All kinds of beasts went in his ark,
And Noah himself came riding by,
And they poked a mean finger at Noah,
But ol' Noah told the ark to move!
To move, move, move!

About a mile away I could hear the night-shift Moon-workers testing radar-equipment. Occasionally, I saw lights flash in the sky, junk in orbit.

But finally the song, the clapping, the warmth of real people (in the church) delivered me to a temporary inner mansion of peace.

I'd caught a glimpse of her through the branches of huge trees with low limbs. Matilda, the yellow girl with a banana face.

She was moving in slow motion. Her colorless sack dress hung on her like the garment of a scarecrow. The uneven traffic of sunlight out of the congress of the clear sky jumped, scattered down all over her, making her brighter than she could possibly be.

> Sometimes I caught sight of her when she paused like a Mantis. She had the same noble, predaceous manner; or, if it was Sunday, daytime, during the break in "service," I'd see her coming up from the girls' peepee hole, which was simply an area behind a cluster of bushes. With other girls, she'd come up the path, upstanding, her yellow eyes glowing like a Manx's. Barefoot even on Sunday, she was poorer than "us." (That "us," by the way, does not include *me*: I had no price!)

I ached for Matilda. I wanted to know her thoughts. I went about all day trying to imagine what her cunt looked like. I kept seeing Veronica's, Gal's, Twinkie's. That was as far as I could get. I really thought I deserved her, but I didn't dare *act* on that sentiment. She was very skinny and on her face always was an uncomplicated, passive expression. Probably she was too "sweet" to have hairs on her thing. I dreamed of making love to her. The more I thought of her the more compassionate I felt. Soon, I was dreaming that she and I were making love *together*. (Quite an improvement over: doing it *to* her).

> There goes your banana-face girl, said B.B.

Matilda was ahead of us, going up the road. If I remember correctly, we were students at that time. I remember carrying books. Yes; we must have been coming from a school. There were other students on the unpaved road, climbing the hill. How we got to be students, how we eventually stopped being students, I don't know. But that is not surprising. I could see her shoulder blades bumping beneath her shabby dress. I loved her small skeletal backside. Even her ass had almost no meat to it, yet I loved it, I loved it. How it moved beneath her dress. When she carried her books against her flat chest. If only I had enough nerve to say something to Matilda! Even *hello* might be enough to sustain me! I'd like to be able to walk right up to her and say something like, let's get married and have babies. But the trouble is I don't really want to marry

100

and have babies. I want to help Moses Westby rewrite the road signs in Nebraska. That's what I really want to do with my life. All the same, I love Matilda. I don't really know what to do about it, though.

I *see* her in my sleep, through *my* eyes.

I see her moving even in her *own* sleep.

That particular night, Grew, B.B., and I went for a walk; leaving church; the old folks singing, inside. Beating their tambourines, cuttin' up somethin terrible!

Down, along the bumpy dirt road Matilda's house faced.

I *dare* you to call her, said Grew.

He won't do it, said B.B.

I *will,* I boasted.

Go on, then!

I dare you, I double dare you! snapped B.B. His square black face glowed in the moonlight. Have you noticed, all faces glow in the moonlight?

Softly (low enough so that she certainly could not hear me) I called across the night, *Matilda, Matilda* . . .

But her soft voice answered. It came from somewhere just beyond the hedge around her house. *Yes?*

I was shocked and frightened.

B.B. and Grew sensed my reaction to her response and began laughing out loud—*at* me. I blushed and stumbled over a rock. I picked myself up and tried to see my way through the remainder of the night.

Glancing toward her house, I saw lights in the windows. I heard the chains of a swing moving. Perhaps she was swinging herself in the swing on her porch. Yes. Now, I saw her shadow moving back and forth against the ground, in a clearing the hedges didn't conceal.

Now is the time, said B.B., if you're serious, go over there and fuck her.

Yeah, said Grew, go on, Junebug, we won't tell nobody.

My name is not Junebug.

What difference does it make? *Go!* Grew shot. He pushed me toward the path leading to Matilda's porch. I held back, trying to fight his hands.

The chains continued to squeak.

Beyond that sound and mixed with the endless sound of crickets was the church revival waves. Also, way away somewhere, a drunk woman was singing the blues. The night was damp and hot. And I continued to resist, digging my "good" shoes into the spaces between the rocks in the road, for balance. B.B. joined Grew and they both tried to push me onto the path leading to the girl I loved. I felt helpless, insane with fear. I was afraid of her, afraid she'd reject me, curse me. But the two of them managed to push me all the way up to the porch where she sat calmly swinging back and forth. I didn't dare look up to see her face. My eyes, anyway, by now, were filled with tears and probably I couldn't have seen her if I'd had the nerve to try.

HERE HE IS MATILDA! shouted B.B.

HE SAYS HE LOOOOOOOOOOVES YOU, MATILDA, HERE HE IS, LOOK AT HIM, MATILDA, LOOK AT HIM BLUSH, MATILDA!

I was down on my knees trying to fight it, to escape. Suddenly, Matilda stopped the swing. I was aware of *that*, somehow.

Quickly, she came to the edge of the porch. Her hands on her hips. She looked quite vicious—the light behind her. I could see her only dimly through my tears. I knew in that moment I'd never again be able to face her. Never, ever!

Grew and B.B. were giggling insanely.

WHAT'D YOU WANT US TO DO WITH HIM? B.B. shouted.

They were holding me by my arms and I was desperately trying to fall flat to the ground, to bury myself, if possible, beneath its surface. But the girl still hadn't said anything. Which was a small comfort.

Matilda, however, quickly put an end to that condition. She spoke. She said, Bring him around to the back.

They followed her, dragging me around her house to the back-yard. There was a light from the kitchen window.

Over here, said Matilda. She stood beside an old ice box.

They dragged me over to it. And she opened the thing. I was twisting and struggling, already imagining they would lock me in, and I would die there.

Matilda opened the ice box and backed herself into it, sit-ting with her knees bent; we could see she wasn't wearing un-derpants. At last, there was her cunt! She held her arms out to receive me. And I was rammed into her.

The door of the ice box was slammed and in its airless interior and total darkness there was the breathing frail presence of the girl of my dreams. Yet, all I could do was cry. I began choking and coughing. The fragrance of her pussy filled the ice box and I continued to babble. I hated myself but I couldn't stop.

A match was struck. I looked into Matilda's face and saw that she really was *not* Matilda. Maybe it was the way the light hit her features, from the bottom. The way she was holding the match. But she looked like *Veronica*. Unbelievingly, I said, Veronica!

She opened the lips of her vagina and a blue butterfly strug-gled out, flapping its wings. It was sticky, and couldn't fly. So, it lay there, in the ice box, between us. It lay on its side. She held the match close to it. It was trying to get up but it could only weakly move its wings.

Later, B.B. and Grew turned me free and I ran blindly to-ward the road. I ran into the hedges. I fell into them. Their dust filled my nose, mouth and ears; as I pulled myself up I was in pain from the scratches received from the narrow limbs. But I ran out of the yard, and up the road toward the church where I heard the old folks singing about somebody called Noah.

Matilda, whom I hate now, is in church today, witnessing my "marriage ceremony."

> They have forced me into it. I hate them *all.* They say I am "cute" but I want to spit in their eye. Sometimes lately I almost have the courage . . .

I thought of running south through the woods. I saw myself running south through the woods until I came to the sea. I stole a boat and paddled until I was exhausted. I lost sight of land. I changed my mind; I was probably midway across. For a moment or two before turning the boat around, I watched the water ripple in the purple evening light.

> But the hard, cold fact *is* I was (now) being forced to marry a bitch I hated. Because everybody, including the bride's father, her mother, her sisters, her brothers, thought the affair so entirely *cute!*

They have squeezed me into a tuxedo. These people are pushing me too far! One day, I feel sure, I'll kill . . . them. I'll kill 'em off like they're flies. This little bitch. They've stuffed her into a flowing white wedding gown. The church is white; its roof, green. It sits at the edge of a muddy, red dirt road. On both sides, a profusion of bushes and trees. And above, there is the surprisingly large, clear daytime sky. My "bride's" name? *Oni.* She's small, yella, with orange eyes, bright black spots in them. Eric Dunn, who fucks horses, is her brother and is the most popular fella in town. The women especially love him for the size of his sexual appendage: it is not small.

> I hold my right arm stiff. Oni places her tiny hand on it. From the beginning of the walkway to the church door we walk, then enter the church, slowly. Eyes on us. Smiling happy faces.

OH AREN'T THEY CUTE!

HEAVENLY!

SUCH DARLINGS!

WOULDN'T IT BE WONDERFUL IF THEY ONE DAY REALLY MARRY!!!

(I know Moses is in the church somewhere but I haven't been lucky enough yet to spot him. He promised he'd come—so he *must* be here!)

Up the aisle we solemnly march, imprisoned. My heart as heavy as hydrogen. The preacher is a round black man in a blue suit. His head is monoclinic shaped and his beady eyes glow behind rimless thick glasses.

We reached the point where we could stop. The rimless eyes glared at us. I looked over my shoulder. Still searching for Moses Westby. There he was.

Like Humphry Bogart in *Petrified Forest*. A tough killer, witnessing an unfortunate matrimonial rite. A woman's heavy hand twists my face back toward my bride and the preacher.

What is Matilda thinking? *Fuck her;* I don't care what she's thinking! She sits between a guard and a delivery woman. B.B. and Grew are seated on Thursday's left, Gal, on the right. On the bench behind them, Nasteylipp has her big thighs crossed and she's smacking a mouth full of gum. For some reason, a state policeman stands rigidly at the entrance, watching everything. A half-grin on his face. It could be in his hand. It's *that kind* of grin.

The monoclinic-headed man is performing the ceremony. Couldn't they show me some clemency sometime? How many levels of imprisonment must I endure?

They make me kiss her. Everybody laughs.

WEEEEEEEEEEEEEEEEEEEEEE they scream.

As we go out the grains of rice hit me in the face. One put out my eye. And the tears start. And the faces continue to scream *but* with laughter.

———————◆———————

But the *way* you just described to me, said the girl, is the way I already know. It's the way I go home each day. What I really want to know is, the girl said, how do I cross where there's *no* crossing, no sign, no direction.

That's the only place you can do it, I told her; at that corner . . . See? into that street, where you live. You just have to break the rule.

She didn't seem to understand. I left her standing there, blank. I continued along the highway, my sun in Capricorn, hot, tired. The sockets of my eyes ached. The joints of my fingers were stiff. Upahead, lying on the roadside path, a shabby bearded white boy had his hand extended toward me. I looked back. The girl had turned off the highway—no doubt, into the woods.

Say buddy, the boy said, you got a nickel?

No.

I need twenty-six cents, he said. A nickel would do it.

Farther up, I saw something that looked like a girl with huge tits, growing out of the cement. She had big, bright happy brown eyes. Her hair was blue-black. On closer inspection I discovered she was not a statue; *no*body made her.

Hello.

She didn't return the greeting.

Have you seen anything? (A voice on my right).

Like what?

We're going to a birthday party. All the kids are coming. Why don't you come . . . ?

106

I want to believe you. What sort of party?

I just told you, a birthday party.

But whose?

Yours; but it was *supposed* to be a surprise. Now, you may not be born.

Moses Westby's new woman is a big juicy pink hunk of flesh. She holds her thighs open with the pressure of her mighty hands. The noses of old men break beneath the elastic spryness of her rump as they sniff the musky perfume of her white funk. Old bats, crazy and bleeding from the eyeballs, scold her. Their mouths drip fluids and dance violently around her, trying to put a spell on her.

I realized I was having a dream.

Moses wakes to go to the toilet to urinate and though he shouldn't have to climb steps to get to the bathroom he does. Actually there are no steps between the bedroom and the bathroom. But he continues to go up, and it's such a blind, pointless ascendancy. He's had more than a bad dream.

He's naked and the light in the toilet is yellow. His color, at the moment, is raw sienna and he has a potgut that looms greenish under the glow.

I dislike his stomach.

Just as he begins brushing his teeth suddenly his new woman emerges from the toilet bowl. A funny place to come from; and she's giggling, as she shakes like a wet dog, at the same time, reaching for Moses. She falls before him and begins gobbling his sex organs with twitching love. Greedy affection. What would Veronica think of this incident? Should she think of it? Should I think of Veronica?

Anyway. Somehow.

The fat pink woman drags Moses from the toilet and into a spaceship where there is *x* number of dials, all of them alike, no names on any. White dots against black strips. Loud ratcheese loudspeakers looming from the walls. Moses looks weak from (perhaps) shock. (I'm sure now that I'm dreaming. I mean, I was sure before, but I'm *so* sure now, there *is* room for doubt . . .)

Like a defeated child's, after a track meet, Moses' head falls between the fat woman's tits. She comforts him, strokes his woolly head.

She hasn't told him her name. Maybe she knows it doesn't matter. It could be a style of wisdom she's in on.

As though she's psychic, she speaks. My name, she says, is anything; honeybunch.

Has Moses become an involuntary astronaut?

He stretches out on something that looks like an operation table. Rather than launching the spaceship the woman lies down beside him, takes him in her arms as though he's an infant. She rocks him gently against her breasts.

From beneath her slip (which is the only thing she's wearing) the head of an infant begins to emerge.

And *I* feel the beginning of an erection.

The gray water rolls in, slaps against the torn wedding gown stranded on the rocks. A woman close to me, I suspect, has died. She was, I think, discovered here, among the rocks, at exactly 5:05. Of course, nothing yet is official. A face; her face. It begins to come up out of the water. The forecast was still cloudy; but there was no lightning. She emerges from the sea, between the rocks. Pieces of moss and cactus plant are hanging from the flimsy wet material. The woman naturally is naked.

> She is singing and the sun is going down in the sea. A huge sadness swells in me, yet I cannot cry. Rather, I am on the verge of laughter.

I once slept with her. Very close. I was *in* her. I came out of and I go back in her.

> The hairs inside her nostrils. I watch them, as I listen to her breathe. I see the hairs moving in and out. When she exhales, I feel her wind. Her breath smells funny. There is a strand of hair growing from her chin. Her lips are dry, cracked. She annoys me whistling through her half-closed mouth while she sleeps.

Pine leaves sweep against the edge of her skull.

> Her eyes open sometimes during her sleep.

It scared the shit outa me to see her eyes open like that one night when I got up to go to the toilet. Thought she was dead. I waited a minute, saw that she was still breathing.

> Her breasts, sad things, are two tiny empty sacks. The bones of her ribcage seem to push up through her thin, pale flesh. Especially the one between her empty sacks.

109

I want to kiss her and stay close to her.

> But I know Moses Westby would not find her interesting nor could he enjoy her sexually. I'm not sure, though, with the four empty houses of his horoscope, he'd find any other *use* for her.

She is lying at the edge of the water now sleeping near the rock where her wedding gown sags. I feel safe, knowing she won't die. Somehow, though, she's as mysterious as that canyon where the Indians took their own lives. (I wish I could take my *own* life and do *something* with it.)

> She's coming back, now.

She bounces back into me like a rubber ball. She's like Veronica. I love her as much. I wish she was Veronica. Maybe she is; but if she is not maybe she will volunteer to *be*come Veronica.

Though I wander and wonder a long while through ripples of wet darkness, void of any sign, with no view of her, when I do finally see her walking through the water, her hair pulled tightly neatly back from her noble face, I know she is walking in her sleep. There's a dreamy look jutting from her. It connects with me. A current. She is traveling through her unconscious planet.

> Sometimes when she snored too loudly I'd kick her softly.

In our relationship the secrecy never bothered me. That it didn't however, *does* bother me. There was between us a certain eroticism, a kind of sanctity, something forbidden. I say these things as though they are closely linked; and they are.

> She generated immense power and I lived in her conscious mind. She instinctively knew all about guilt, justice, mercy, morality, children, language, and incest. *Yes*, incest. (But it wasn't incest —*we would have gone insane had we not entered each other*.)

Unlike Moses, she had no close knowledge of hustling and the simple business of getting along, which sometimes fills the mind with a detailed knowledge of sex, violence, murder, and racism. Especially racism. This lack of social awareness explains *why* she's ended up here, in the sea, ruined. It also explains the torn wedding gown.

I took the carnation flower out again and kissed it.

I moved closer, to get a better look.

She gets tangled up in her own hair if the tide is high and beats her too hard. But so far, she's been lucky. She gets sick, weak, but she overcomes every spell, every attack, and she survives her own greed.

I see Veronica move, a shadow, against the cool foggy sunrise. (She certainly isn't Miss Dimplebutt nor Miss Pussywillow, so why not assume I have her name psyched out correctly . . . ?)

The planks beneath the water, her feet touch bottom. She smiles. It's a distant, vacant smile. (Even by a penal code, a dream, though perhaps not a very pretty dream is, nevertheless, possible. The frail trip of cool minds bumping around the staging of the Aquarius constellation—like clumsy, fat angels. False hopes, trick dreams, warm time, and wet space. I expect no change . . . at the moment of the retrograding vernal equinoctial shift into 30 degrees of the Aquarius setup. *No change;* except that which I forge.) If I could see her pink feet beneath the water they would *be* purple. Just for my eye. The window wet from the rain outside. The curtain pulled back to show the mind simply how dreary the day is. Sometime she will sit up in bed and bury her face between her knees and cry about money.

We're rich, just remember, we're *very* rich: we've never been poor!

Many times she spoke such strange words. She wasn't really an angel—angels have dicks. Her strangeness forstalled questions. And therefore, answers. Like how can I explain how she managed to *be* in bed asleep and at the same time, go to the bathroom to pee?

The question I probably can never answer is: why did I *need* to find him. (He'd tried to murder Veronica, remember; then, he'd disappeared behind one of his many names or some other façade; I'd survived weird highways, I was weary; fascinated by light, I'd stumbled blindly through many many meaningless bright rooms; and my memory still isn't very good; but when I tell a lie about what happened I *do* know, precisely, the degree to which it is a lie—not that it is any help to you; then, you remember, how Veronica left me to die, that summer, at the footsteps of Thursday's lack of mercy? The good things I managed to get my hands on then I still possess: like the carnation and the wrappers from the candy bars the soldiers threw at us; even things not good for me to keep I find difficulty throwing out—like the blond wig forced on my head by the traveling salesman; no; after all that has happened it does puzzle me a bit that I am still *concerned* and puzzled.)

> If Moses Westby wasn't in one place, certainly he'd have to be in another. With "lightskirts," like some semi-hip bishop of 1597?

He used to stand on street corners grinning at nothing. Yeah. Or rapping with the cats. All of their black, greasy faces hung just a little out of respect for his tall money.

> His money, his skill with dice and cards, and his Cadillac—a new one every year!

Not only can I not find his shadow I cannot find even the cool spot on the earth where it lingered against something, away from the sun. It could be a clue; but clues often turn out as shabby as worn-out socks wet inside shoes. Yet, I can't make it standing still.

I climbed a killerdiller hill. If it were Friday and if I were to see him he'd be wearing overalls. Friday, the workingman's payday, was his most profitable day. While whipping the game on them Moses felt it only right to dress as they dress. So, this was the one day he didn't wear his expensive kicks and fronts.

> I stopped at the top of the hill. Realizing I really wasn't at the top, nevertheless, I couldn't move on. Where was that sap-sucker? "If ANYBODY ask you what I do," Moses once said to me, "tell 'em I run a coal yard, I operate a gas station; tell 'em I'm in the dry cleaning business, but don't *never* tell 'em the truth—!"

I'd thought of looking in the coal yard in the gas station in the dry cleaners but . . . why should I? He himself had told me he was somewhere else. So, I *had* to move on.

> There's some promise that wasn't fulfilled. But what promise? And why does it necessarily still exist? Can it be moved? Can I stop asking questions? Should questions themselves stop forming?

I stand on this bluff at a fork. The road that crosses leads (I think) to Buttermilk Bottom. The morning sunlight shines over the edge of the red-brick school building that waves a spanking brand-new American flag. Dusty green trees dance around the structure.

I start walking down toward Buttermilk Bottom. People come toward me. Old black women carrying paperbags, their uniforms, their lunches. Going to factories or domestic gigs. Dead eyes. Two or three men among them. The men are clad in coveralls. Lunchbuckets. But threading their way through these uphill climbers are hundreds of children, yellow, tan, black, and gold, descending toward the school building, which looms just beyond Buttermilk Bottom.

> Sudden(ly).

As I start down, all the people (men women children) come to a standstill, like a still in a boss film.

> I stand still, now.

What're we waiting for?   Hitler?   An air raid? My answer does not come. But what they all do jumps like photostatic copy into my brain cells. The shock (in me) is cool but

113

also like having a fifty-gallon tub of ice water thrown from a fifteenth floor into my face: each one has stopped beside a tree. Many trees, obviously, line the sides of the road. They each lift a leg (dog fashion) and blast a stream of steaming hot piss against a tree. Even the females piss like male dogs. Why are they *dogs?* Nature operates to promote itself—even through "man-made" fertilizer?

However.

It doesn't strike me. It strikes me as odd only after it's over. And each is moving as before. As though there had been *no* break in the rhythm they set. They *re*set a weary rhythm.

> Just before I hit Buttermilk Bottom Slick John Flower comes racing down in his T-Model Ford. He came out of a sidestreet near the school and headed straight for the Buttermilk Bottom intersection. If I hadn't jumped over into the bushes on the side he would have surely run over me. If he'd heard what under my breath I called him he'd have tried to wash out my mouth with soap.

He sees me. He stops. The car door opens. Get in, says Slick.

> I was looking for Moses Westby.

Fuck em—he ain't never done nothing *for* you! *Get in!*

> I hate school, I said.

Who *said* anything about school! Slick snapped.

> But if I *get in* that's where you'll take me.

Slick was silent as he studied my face. He held his head sideways and watched me from the corners of his eyes.

> Slick finally spoke. Well, he said, go up that hill there. You have a cousin you've never seen who lives at the end of that row of houses on the left. His name is T-Bone. If he don't know . . . nobody knows!

Clanging and rattling, Slick drives off into the sunrise. I feel better *already!*

Trying to see through the dusty screen into T-Bone's home, I stand on his front porch. The truth is I stand *under* and *near*

114

more than *on*. But this was one of those rare occasions. (Inside) all I could see from where I stood was a white cloth on a dresser and a rocking chair's edge, caught by sunlight from a side window. I called out, *Cousin T-Bone!*

I heard the squeak of footfalls on floorboards somewhere in the back. I listened intently.

Then, intensely, I saw my new cousin coming. An old man came creeping up to the door.

Yes?

A round, very old black face; a gap between his teeth. Skull full of white hair.

I'm Moses Westby.

That you, Junebug?

Moses.

Hanh?

My name—

Cousin T-Bone opened his screen door. Pointed toward the tool shed. Over there, the old man said. T-Bone's finger shook.

What's over there?

He's out there, in the shed. Go on out there.

I am filled sudden(ly) with fear.

T-Bone closed and locked his screen door and went back deep into his house and I to his shed.

Looked in. There he was. At first, I didn't know him for who he really was. He was tiny, his body was that of an infant. "Christ child in a manger." Chewing straw, there were cows looking over a plank down upon him. At their feet, chickens pecked and clucked. Then, why did T-Bone call it a tool shed? It had always before now been a toolshed. Unusual things happen.

Moses Westby's head was as big as a man's (or, as big as it usually is) and he was gray as a face in the movies. I was slowly recognizing him.

115

I sensed it was taking him longer to get to me.

Looking up, he'd seen me but no recognition reflected.

I'm the inspector, I said. You used to guard me. You once took me to a stock-car race. Remember . . . ?

He was sucking his thumb and twiddling his toes. A very thoughtful expression held camp in his face.

Oh, yes! Moses finally said. How could I forget?

He smiled. I always loved his smile. And suddenly I remembered how once two plainclothesmen had come bringing him home in handcuffs so he could say a few last-minute words to Veronica and us. Then, they took him away to solitary confinement. Why did I remember that *now?*

You're Moses, he said.

Yes, and you're Moses—right?

A dark shadow fell across his face. He spoke softly, doubtfully. I don't know, he said. When I think about hitting the trail again I think I'm Ley Orpet. This morning I called myself Luke Snott—felt just that bad.

I wanted to cry I felt so sorry for him. Yet I knew pity wasn't what he needed. Not now   .not*ever.*

If you had a camera, he said, grinning, you could take my picture.

Nasteylipp has a brownie camera.

Who's Nastylip?

Lucy "Greenhalge" Flower.

Being a good sport he chuckled like I knew he would.

Where's your Cadillac?

That thing? I lost it.

I didn't know what to say to Moses. A moment of silence. Then I spoke. Moses, I said, remember that time when the angel's bride drove you out with a broom?

A fucking dyke, he hissed. No, I don't remember. I'm sleepy. I want to sleep, now. Why don't you come back later?

The edge of his face breaks into a half smile as he reaches for my hand.

Thursday was doing her "thing" in the kitchen. And it was noon. As they say, she was burning. Stoking the stove, she used the stoker. Every ten minutes or so she checked the sizzling and juicy pork roast way in the back of the black hot oven. A slow cook. This meal would be the center of a special occasion. Staying out of her way, I watched her a moment, before running out back.

For the first time since his stroke Grady was going to sit at the table and eat with other people—us.

But which incidents are worth remembering . . . ?

It is the time of the "special occasion." Old Grady, Thursday herself, Grew, B.B., Gal, and myself. The kitchen table is the focal point.

Looking at Grady: I had always been young, now—suddenly, I was old! Just from looking at him!

Halfway through the weird gathering Grady spit a wad 'a food back into his plate. Clearing his mouth so he could speak.

When you talk to me, Grady said to Thursday, talk straight . . . You know *I* know *who* and *what* you are. And you know, Grady continued, I don't fall for none of that screaming and calling on God! You black evil bitch *you hussy!* Remember! I picked your black scheming ass off the streets of New Orleans in your voodoo days—

My voodoo days?

You heard me, bitch! Grady groaned. The damnest fool thing I ever in all my life done . . . !

What? asked Thursday.

Marrying you, *that's* what!

> Grady gripped the arms of his wheelchair. He looked for a moment like a man having a stroke. (*Another* stroke.)

NOW LOOK AT ME! Grady demanded. *I'm a broken ol' man in a wheelchair and helpless! It's all your fault!*

> Thursday carefully wipes her thick hands on her apron, while keeping her eyes focused on her plate.

Grady's heavy, angry breathing fills the kitchen. I watched him dip his cold toast into his coffee. He was sloppy. Coffee ran down his chin as he tried to stuff the whole piece of bread into his face. And he was in the middle of a spasm. His blue eyes climbed, taking in her face. She was perhaps the spitting image of some female monster he once feared . . . But *who* was she . . . ?

> Grady's toothless mouth worked furiously at the soggy bread. His back was badly bent. His hair and nails were filthy. He ate like eating was a secret rite or like one afraid that spirits would through food possess his soul. A careful though spittle-dripping and knotted man. I remembered quickly and sharply and sadly his long wrinkled appendage with its weird cabbage hanging from its head. Why, old man, why? What *un*resurrectable rhythms hide in you? How did you, a white man in a white nation, end up living and dying such a black death? With his brains he should have been directing the Manned Spacecraft Center uptheroadapiece.

Later.

> Stand still, you evil woman, and listen to me! said Grady. He wiped his wet mouth with the back of his arm. Thursday, he said, his voice dropping sadly, the evening shadows giving his face a sunken, hollowed appearance, Thursday, he said again; I . . . don't . . . think . . . I'm . . . much . . . longer . . . for . . . t-this . . . w-world . . .

The old man was clearly crying. Tears dropped into his finely chopped pork roast—which he'd had trouble chewing.

> Don't talk like that, Thursday said, with lowered eyes. Only God knows them things.

There's one request, ne said.

She looked at him.

B.B. coughed. Grew's feet, beneath the table, shuffled. I saw that Gal's mouth was stuffed and her eyes closed in the effort to chew her possession. (God! Who'd ever want Carnal Knowledge of *her*?!)

I think Thursday was holding her breath. Her crusty hands folded over her apron. The kitchen was still hot from the oven heat and I wondered at least once why we weren't eating in the dining room.

Just one request, Grady repeated. I know you ain't never been faithful to me, ain't never showed no kinda respect for my wishes, but after I'm gone, please, *please*, all I ask of you is *don't sleep with no niggers*. Now, I know you've been doing it all these years we've been together. And I've sorta made excuses for it cause of your nationality—telling myself, well, after all, Thursday herself is *not* white . . .

You don't make sense to me, Grady, she said.

I guess we ain't never been able to talk to each other.

It's cause you talk crazy, man! You talk about dying and worrying about who I'm gonna be fucking after you die. And God knows screwing is the last thing on my mind. Don't you realize I'm way past the change of life?

Grady spat a wad of slimy food back into his plate.

Gal snickered. It was catching.

Shut up and eat! snapped Thursday.

Later.

His mouth was moving. He was almost asleep. He spoke. Thursday, tomorrow, I want to put on a clean shirt and eat at the table again. Okay?

They brought him back to the house in a casket and he was puffed up and without color but in a black suit he looked for the first time like somebody important and now it was too late to look that way. His face was full as though he had teeth and the ruffles in the casket were pure silk. He looked like the bud in the center of a bloodless flower.

I couldn't stop looking at his lips. I kept expecting to see them move. And, of course, they did move, and he spoke. But what he said wasn't clear.

Though his eyes were closed they wouldn't stay closed. He kept opening them, he kept looking around. It was against the "rules" and, the old bastard, he knew it! but apparently he wanted to see what was going on. When first I saw his eyes pop open they scared the shit out of me. I ran through the house, about to bust. But I didn't dare. Thursday, anyway, always said "we" made a enough noise to "wake up the dead"!

Thursday apparently closed his eyes, cause the next time I saw him (later the same day) his lids were down.

They were going to bury him Sunday in the sunlight across the road in the graveyard. Well, that was possibly where he should have been put a long time ago.

Grady's physical remains were in state in the house while we waited for others close in name to come to take part in the funeral rites.

Hands folded on his chest. Lifeless knuckles, dead cells.

The crust of his lips, flies were busy at their edges. They buzzed and buzzed, trying to enter. They never seemed satisfied with what they got from the dry surface of his lips. And when they tried to fly away after giving up they bumped the silky veil discovering they were trapped. They couldn't remember how they'd gotten in so they had to buzz around the veil until by accident they escaped.

It was very interesting watching him dead. At least this way when he talked you didn't have to listen to his words.

The second and third day it was the same thing: the flies kept trying to pry into his mouth. On the third day one eye came all the way open. One fly stood on the open eye's lid and cleaned his legs. He did it slowly and carefully. I wondered why flies stop and why they start again. What motivates them, anyway? What sorta diptera lust resides in that muscidae need to penetrate the dead area of a *solid* where the atoms are packed close . . . ?

Sometimes they spent all day crawling in nervous patterns (that made a strange sense) across his cheeks, up the hill that was his nose, down it, around it; but they also spent a lot of time fucking with the flowers around the coffin in which the casket sat. As time took up space just happening the flowers lost their freshness and their odor deepened and grew intensely sharp, almost harsh, but not unbearable like jimson or ragweed. The flies, too, dug them less as they lost their tenderness. By the morning of the fourth day all of this and so much else that I cannot ever find words to convey was evident. There was, however, something erotic about Grady's death, generated from but not necessarily dependent on nor limited by the presence of his remains. I mean, if his body had not been in the house, his death might still have emitted sexuality, and a certain over-whelming and incomprehensible obscenity or dislocated sanctity. You know what I mean.

Grady's face was dry and it was heavily powdered. It wasn't that he had lost any charm through death but as a witness to his death I had managed to invest him for the first time with a charm that contained even a sort of exuberance he never before (in my frame of reference) qualified for. And this had nothing to do with a licentious image of any kind.

Surely, the fact that it had taken him many years to die had something to do with the lack of grief. The relief, clearly, sprung from a shared feeling that his discontinuation was at least tacitly considered a kind of Christian blessing.

> As those close to him in name (and a few who possibly felt sympathetic remembering him when he was young and in good health in the days when he was a brilliant architect with sharp esthetic taste, and many people were flocking to him) came now, again, his deeds, all that could be remembered, all that were respectable to remember, were being voiced. Death has a cynical though emotionally erotic effect that is explosive always inside the enormous mystery of the taboos surrounding it. So, not just the "close" ones talked; people like Fisheye, Ginger-cake Lovely Flower, Yella Coo Margaret Flower, Sugar Girl Valerie Flower, Hain Alcock, Twinkie, Dischel, Papanek, a few of Mister Hallet's family survivors, that racist truck driver, a few of Matilda's relatives though not Matilda herself; the angel's bride surprised everybody by also coming all the way from the city; many old guards, delivery women and a district attorney was there; there was a warden there who, it was said, had been Grady's best friend during childhood, when Grady was living strictly as a white person, getting a very fine white education. Of course, Moses Westby and Veronica (Flower) Westby were there. They, of course, were the two I'd been mainly waiting to see. And now that they were both here in the house on the road facing the graveyard I couldn't find in myself words nor lend to my joy a method of communication.

There were so many cars the driveway couldn't hold them all. People were all over the place, in the house, in the back yard, the front yard, in the driveway between the cars, sitting in the cars, leaning against the cars, strolling out across the fields, walking along the highway; it was a warm crisp Sunday morning and many fresh flowers had been added to the stale ones. I wondered if Nasteylipp's American Chinese gravedigger would show up, and how about her Puerto Rican classical pianist? Nasteylipp, of course, was in the kitchen, helping Thursday fix food. All these folks had to eat, after all! There was an Irish shoeshine boy there who had his shoeshine box with him. But since he seemed interested only in shining shoes and in the price of the grand piano (which Thursday would never even consider selling) I didn't suspect he was the one Nasteylipp had long ago had an affair with. The one she'd known had to be by now older than this kid was. There was an Oriental-looking guy

123

there but I seriously doubt if he was a Japanese-American pop singer. We had no radio in the house but two or three people had on radios in cars and we were getting a mixture of anti-sexual Tin Pan Alley and politically oriented rock. Cigarette, cigar smoke, perfume, and body sweat were excessive everywhere.

> Veronica and Moses Westby sat side by side in Moses' glossy black Cadillac. They were speaking quietly to each other. I couldn't decide whether I wanted to split them up, sit between them, embrace them both, or run under the house and stay there till *all* these imposing people left. I kept walking around the house with my hands in my pockets. Women mostly tried to stop me to rake their fingers through my locks. But I refused to talk to them. I was waiting . . .

I didn't know what I was expecting to happen. Grady was already dead and I'd seen a burial before. Though I'd never before seen anybody "close" to me let down into the ground still a burial was quite simply a burial.

> I went into the kitchen for a drink of water and witnessed Papanek (in slacks and a little drunk) trying to coerce Thursday into selling her the "marvelous" antique cupboard in the dining room. Gingercake, Thursday's oldest ward, had smilingly come to Thursday's defense.

Grady would turn over in his grave, said Gingercake from her round gingercake-colored face, if Thursday *sold* any of these items in this house. Papanek, they spent years collecting these things and nobody on earth's gonna come in here and twist Thursday's arm in a effort to make her sell. If it happens, said Gingercake, it'll be over my dead body!

> Papanek gave her a drunk grin, and with nothing more to say, turned and snapped her head a little in mock shock then went out toward the dining room where the whiskey was.

I was leaving the kitchen, too; and Papanek saw me. *Oh,* she sang, *there you are!*

> And she grabbed me by the shoulder and pulled me against her hip. It was a very bad move. She spilled some of the nasty stuff from her glass on my face and dirty cotton shirt.

You cute thing you!

I'm not a thing, I said. Let me go!

What's the matter—don't you *like* me?

Her breath stank.

I pulled away and shot out the back doorway.

I don't remember their taking his body away; it must have
happened during a night while I was asleep. They took him
away to embalm his body with balsams out of respect for some
excessive and mystic custom that is ego-oriented, in an attempt
to preserve by use of chemicals that which is obviously unpre-
servable. But nevertheless embalmers in the area had always
been among the most successful businessmen. I remembered the
hollowed bird that contained Grew's prick. Why did I remember that now? Doesn't matter. They drain all the blood out of
the veins then pump the veins full of embalming fluid. They
stuff his asshole and mouth who knows perhaps even the other
openings, too.

Lil Miss Liza Jane, remember her grave   ?

She used to dance over her husband's grave at midnight. Naturally, that was before she possessed or rather before one possessed her. Then, even after they were buried side by side
rumor had it that she came out in the full moon and still
skipped about on it to some private melody. Grew said she
was a spirit but B.B. insisted that she was a eurynome; but
that was hardly true since such wolflike creatures who feed on
corpses when not princely sitting on the skin of a vulture have
always (as far as I know) been more male than female. One
thing I will grant, she very possibly had two eyeballs in each
socket—because, I remember nights sitting on the front-porch
in the swing and seeing enchanting lights glowing from the
cemetery in the area where Miss Liza Jane and her husband
were honored by tombstones. And those lights had effects lightning bugs could never manage. I know I manage to convey a
belief in weird things and at the same time a kind of scien-
tific knowledge that would preclude such mental activity. It is
true—I see only the clumsiest "order" anywhere; believe in
nothing really, which is solid reason why I can afford a belief
in all manner of "folly." If I say one thing and feel another,
it's not uncommon. If I believe something and tell you I don't
or vice versa what you do with the paradox is your part of the

bargain. Remember? This was always a seesaw; though not a teeterboard of endless pleasure. In fact, it is the most painful situation I've ever found myself looking from.

But more important than anything so far stated, Grady's death gave me a vision of my own liberation.

Yes. *Yes,* indeed.

I got a glimpse into the possibility of how death of entities with sensibilities can also serve the discontinuous nature of all life. It almost hypnotized me, the message was so profound and potentially useful. It caused a vertiginous effect in my psyche but I was far from dizzy. It was a thin line.

The links were there but they did not really link any of us. We were each still quite diminutive when you bothered to think about our late arrival on earth and the real probability that the globe would endure long after we've checked out. But why do I bother to even give *it* space?

People in the area had always claimed they could hear ghosts moving around during the night. Dead folks were said to be some restless motherfuckers. The ones who'd died "before their time" or in *un*natural ways, especially those. They came back, it was said, to get even with enemies still alive. It was a way, I think, live people used to check themselves, to (restrict and) atone, to pay for their "sins." Night was not simply the time of death it was also the time of birth and therefore it was never quite clear to me why the ghosts came out in the absence of sunlight causing dogs and maddogs to howl til daybreak.

The big question on everybody's mind (I suspected) was: would Grady (who'd suffered so much and so long) seek the complex and elusive revenge of a ghost. To Thursday, I suspected this question, and other related problematical questions, meant a lot and on her mind weighed quite heavily. When I think of "weight" though, my mind gets into elements like francium or bismuth but I won't bother you with such shit. I'm trying to be lean, if not beautiful.

The preacher is stupid, obviously. Yet the people standing around him with mouths open seem awed. But preachers in this area have always been very popular, like, in other areas, revolutionaries are so frequently the center of much fuss and bootlapping.

In the middle of trying to look quite solemn this particular cocoa-colored preacher constantly explodes into a grin. If I didn't know better I'd swear he was up on grass or laughing gas. He's a fat, short man in a black suit and he's proudly sporting one of those Amos derbies.

I'm sitting on the front step.

Sugar Girl Valerie sits against the wall on the porch bent double in a straw chair weeping. Her dainty handkerchief is drenched. And I'm wondering if I could give her my shirt to use without offending...

I walk over to the Cadillac, lean against it, pretending I'm a cowboy. I have a straw in my mouth.

I hear Veronica say to Moses, He was old. It had to come. I loved him, he loved me and I don't feel guilty. He was good to me even though I wasn't his by birth like the others were.

I wondered at that statement. *Wasn't his what?* I can't probe it, now. The funeral ritual quality pervades the air.

Several days ago Slick dug the hole the coffin will be lowered into. It took him three days of unrelenting toil. At first Thursday had insisted that B.B., Grew, and I help, but Slick didn't want our help. This, with tears in his eyes, was *his* task.

What a lovely dress, somebody said.

Thank you.

A transfer truck groans by.

The ambulance driver sits on the fender of the ambulance picking his teeth with a toothpick. I wondered where he got the toothpick—all my life I'd wanted one. One of my main ambitions was to one day get a hold of a toothpick, a *real* one. The driver is a black scarecrow of a man in a chauffeur's bibbed cap. He gazes silently at the ground. A colony of ants work in their natural desperate way where his eyesight falls.

> (After Slick had finished digging the grave yesterday he'd taken a weed saw and chopped away the tallest weeds cluttering the path to the churchless graveyard. So, today, as they followed the pallbearers, the people would not get their legs scratched. The path had been made easy, and Slick, now, went about proudly telling everybody of his work for this occasion. He, too, suffered grandly, I would surmise, from questions concerning what Grady would now do after death. And possibly the reason he hadn't wanted any help with digging the grave and weeding the path is pretty obvious.)

Four men. They came out of the house carrying the casket on long palls. People all about fell silent and fell in line behind them.

> The preacher led the way across the highway.

We all entered the weeded path and climbed toward the graveyard. The procession was quite solemn with some outbursts mostly from the women. Thursday, however, walking with a black veil over her face, clad in a long black dress, hightop black shoes, was absolutely silent—not a tear.

> The coffin had already been placed in the hole so that now the pallbearers had only to let down the casket into the pinewood coffin. The pinewood smelled fresh from the sawmill. And the sawmill wasn't far away.

I feel that what I've been waiting to see and feel will never happen since this is *not* it.

Why does this affair have to be so brutally solemn? I want to go running away into the woods and play with snails or grass-hoppers. I want to go, lie on my stomach, and watch ants work against the coming of hard times. I want to try to snatch the sunlight spilling down through the leaves of the trees in the forest. But no.

In my crisp suit I walk beside Veronica and Gal beside Moses. It was obvious neither Veronica nor Moses was happy and though I felt they each deserved happiness I didn't and I still don't have a wild enough imagination to invent mates for them especially since, during a funeral procession, to assume that a sexual partner is the main source of adult happiness is in itself a bit impolite no matter *how* precise it is to the *true* nature of sex and the true *nature* of death. But then, my po-liteness has always been very superficial. I wish I could explain why, but you'll simply have to try to understand *why* the nat-ural way.

The casket is suspended over the grave and the preacher talks. *This man,* he says, *is going to heaven! Yes, Lord!* He done suffered a long time and he deserves heaven!

As they lowered the casket into the ground female whimpering and sobbing and wailing got louder. I was watching Thursday. And Thursday never even sniffed her nose. Nor closed her eyes.

I dreamed that Moses was my father and the stars were shining above the brick walls of his prison cell. The iron gates were dull arms against its hard shadows.

But on Moses' face there was a soft smile. A smile that said, I knew I wouldn't win but it doesn't matter, because *in me* where it really matters, *I win* anyhow.

And Moses has a gun. The guard on duty doesn't yet know Moses has a gun.   My guess is, he plans to liberate that which, from his point of view, is *the self;* then, possibly, come back and bravely reclaim us, his desperate wards.

Click, says the gun Moses holds toward the prison guard's skull.

Okay sucker! screams Moses, sounding very much like a tough movie star. Take this! BLAM! And this! BLAM! And this! BLAM!

The guard fell over the static railing and plopped on the antiseptic floor, five, maybe six flights down. The whole place was battleship gray and it stank of cleanliness.

Meanwhile, it occurs to Moses that he's still confined. After all, the keys that could free him went over the rail on the hip of the turnkey.

Shortly, all the other prisoners wake up and begin booing or cheering him. Some beat their teeth against the bars while others growl. Several commit suicide in the midst of the noise. This is nothing unusual in a prison.

The problem was, Moses couldn't get out of the cellblock without jumping over the railing into his death. That was the only alternative to going back into his cell. Any moment now the warden and a flood of guards would probably pour in on him with tear gas or a shower of bullets.

Some people had demonstrated how they could adjust to a penal system but few had made peace with a stone prison within a prison.

Shit! I wondered, Why didn't Moses think to shoot the lock off the fucking door—? Ya' know, like the cowboys.

Sure, but suppose one of the bullets ricochet, backfire, hit him between the eyes, or knock out his front buck teeth, or worse, come to rest like a bee in a flower, inside his skull?

Meanwhile, the getaway car is outside. Veronica is at its wheel and she looks like a vogue chick out of the 1940s—you'd think she was Lizabeth Scott. She toots her horn impatiently as though she's not going to dare wait much longer. Already sticking her pretty neck out, doing this outside a prison within a prison.

Maybe something went wrong, Veronica thinks.

By now Moses Westby hears a thousand footfalls coming into the cellblock. They've discovered the body of the dead guard? What'd you do at a moment like this? Do you try to convince 'em you were just kidding around? or do you duck for protection behind the magic of an amulet? (but what if you don't have an amulet and what if spells and incantations are beyond your scope   ?)

The moment they see Moses and see he has a gun all of them start firing on him.

Filled with their metal, he gags, stumbles, drops his gun, a classic stunt. Just before he falls he peeps out of his cell window. Lizabeth Scott, who happens to be looking up at that moment, winks, makes the peace symbol, steps on the gas, and drives off. Knowingly and perhaps any moment now (because she can't see where she's going for the tears clouding her eyes), she will join him.

While I thought that losing Veronica and Moses would end me it has operated to give me a tough inner core.

I was leading Oni Dunn through the dingy and segmented barracks of a high school because I'd promised to show her something. And she trusted me. And I trusted myself. But I'd wanted to accomplish the mission without being seen by the vicious authorities. I'd promised her that if she could follow closely and not get lost, I'd show her the forest on the other side of the highway, beyond the graveyard. It would give her some idea of how the earth looked just before man came to occupy it; but Oni got lost in a sudden outpouring of students from one of the barracks.   So, I arrived at the edge of the forest alone. And the first thing I saw was a tourist wandering around with a camera on a strap around his neck. I couldn't see the guy's face, yet I had the distinct feeling I knew him. I'm sure I recognized the movements of his body.   Then abruptly out of the forest emerged a red pickup truck with Oni (of all people! in duplicate!) standing up in its back-end. And she was shouting WEEEEEEEEEEEEEEEE and from her right hand (which was held high over her lovely head) flowed a rivulet of bright-green powder, spreading against the sky.

Where am I going? I know where I've come from.

Somebody owns each thing. Who owns me? It changes, the ownership, I mean. But my shit, while I hold on to it, I own it; even if somebody else (at any given moment) happens to possess the titleship to me the shit in me remains my secret. The owner might not even suspect it's there unless I'm subjected to x-ray. But even in the meanest sections of the penal system the authorities seldom go so far as to examine prisoners so closely.

Another thing I'm fast discovering to be mine and mine alone. It's my dick. Though there isn't very much I can do, I can do whatever I want with it.

> I am a man. I am Moses. I am a child. I am Moses. Moses has a huge eye that looks out; with it he tries to see everything. He has a flat, wide nose and an oval plate crammed between his gums and his bottom lip. A sculptured skull. Inside his head, I look out of his wise eyes, see the same world he sees. In detail. All the rooms of his being are airtight and sound-proof.

Sometimes I feel like a cat blindly scratching my way through the netted fishhooks and rusty barbed wire of amnesia. Even if I were somewhere throwing myself fully into something the bad memory would remain. I know. It's frustrated because of the real things and incidents I might enjoy remembering; and don't tell me about the theory that the mind does away with what it can't handle.

Veronica. She holds me carefully against her shoulder. It is all very dim. Yet, the essence of it is with me. I feel the excitement of screaming people—thousands of them! They are all looking *up*. What's up there?   Ah! A famed man riding a bicycle high against the sky on a tightrope. The people around us are packed shoulder to shoulder. You'd think they were sending a man to Mars. I lay my cheek against Veronica's neck. Confetti floats through the brisk spaces of the day. Blocks of buildings stand up, their edges, forms, blotting out segments of the skyline. Way way up there the tiny man actually peddles along across the rope with the grandest ease. And nothing else happens. No matter how hard I try, I cannot connect it with anything. It is like something out of an old newspaper, if anything.

Nevertheless, Moses did not go to Mount Sinai for nothing.

3

to
mount
meru

The skill to make paper boats that will sail smoothly across a puddle without getting soggy.   What a worthy goal! I have not forgotten it.

> But the distance from one side of a puddle to the other is not far enough. The problem creates pressure.

Yet, it is not the most daring thing Moses Westby achieved. Be my witness.

BLAM

BLAM

BLAM

Like somebody dynamiting. Then, the slow, steady lifting waves of what sounds like a nearby mob. Screaming. I open the door. Go into the hallway, there's a muddy light from the window in the ceiling.

> The wild odor of blood

and gun powder

> I stand close to the wall.   What
> is   happening   ?

Then. Now.

> In a convulsive effort to catch her breath, Veronica, wobbling like a large pregnant animal, came stumbling into the hallway, clad in a flowing white bathrobe, her hair in curlers. Her white face was bloated and streaked with tears; and she was babbling strangely. Barefoot, her head thrown back, running like something suddenly gone blind.

Still gasping, she stopped at the top of the stairway. Spittle hung from her mouth.

Wondered if she'd been shot. There was no sign.

I shouted, *Veronica!*

And started to run to her when I saw the tip of a double-barreled Winchester shotgun emerge from the doorway.

I ain't going to see you suffer no more, NONE OF YOU! Moses whimpered as he held the firearm. Aiming it at Veronica.

His eye, on this side, squinted. The finger on the trigger.

I screamed his name over and over.

The handle against his left shoulder. The other hand on the metal. His bushy hair standing straight up, uncombed. Potgut, sad black man, in T-shirt, suspenders and no shoes.

I still couldn't believe this was really happening. But he was serious! He pulled the trigger.

My sight jumped from his jerking finger to Veronica. And in that same instant I ran to her, tried to throw myself between her and death. To catch the bullet with my own flesh and thereby show them both how much I loved them.   BLAM BLAM   BLAM

But Veronica's head suddenly splashed open. Chunks of flesh, skullbone, slime, blood, hair. Like a rabbit's body shot at close range. She just sort of veered, even with no head, caught the banister and went over and down.

The frantic mob jammed all sides. We were wedged in the middle. Their curiosity was quite morbid—they watched carefully.

I watched him, his back now to them, only a few feet from their sensuous torment. His lips were moving. What was he saying and to whom was he speaking?

The gun, relaxed. He was looking up now toward the light coming down. Then, he turned and saw me. His smile was sad, extremely bland.

In the very next moment, however, he seemed to be looking beyond me, toward something in himself.

138

When he turned around, he saw Gal standing in her nightgown in the doorway. With the tip of the weapon against her small chest he gave a very affectionate prod. He whispered gently to her; tears running down his cheeks.   All around, people everywhere, watching, shuffling, whispering. It was late afternoon and there was almost no sunlight left at any window for the inside.

I was in shock.

My thoughts necessarily are afterthoughts. Why had I let Moses kill so lovely a woman—why did I let him kill *any*body?

In any case, what on earth had Veronica done to deserve that sort of death on a Sunday morning in a Christian country? But who ever *deserves* death? I had to realize that what one deserved or didn't deserve had nothing to do with death.

Overwhelmed, a few drops of urine dripped from my penis down into my drawers. One drop, with more force than the others, went zigzag down to my knee and paused. I held my muscles. I knew I was in the middle of something too tremendous for words. My asshole was tight with fear and my head was splitting. Furious sensations stabbed and surged through me. Inch by inch I moved along the wall.

Had he deliberately left me outside?

I reached the door; twisted my head only a fraction of an inch. I was gasping trying to hold my breath. I wanted to stop breathing and I didn't know why.

Then I stuck out my head and looked fully in. There was only a little sunlight left and it came dimly through the unwashed window beyond him. His back to me, he was sharply etched against the light. Moses had the shotgun under his arm and was wrestling with Gal who was biting his hands and kicking him as hard as she could. I was torn between an impulse to help her, to help him, and to run.

Children were huddled against the window watching.

The big shabby room stank of piss and burned food and blood and gun powder. In a widening circle of blood, on the floor in a corner, stomach down, arms twisted under, was the body of Twinkie. But why Twinkie? Her back side was a mass of blood and on her face was an expression of release.

Moses suddenly grabbed Gal firmly and flipped her and her head hit the floor. He held her upsidedown by her legs. The shock of it obviously held her silent.

I was not unaware of my own strong need to go check Veronica's body, simply to touch it, to make sure, in awe of death; but for some reason I could not yet pull away. The reason was more than something vague.

Between his legs I saw Gal's comic face.

Moses propped his bare foot against her chest to hold her still, yet she kicked and squirmed.

A man behind me said, I'm gonna take that gun. I won't stand by and see this happen!

Another voice answered, He'll shoot you, you fool!

I wondered, where was the angel's bride. If she was here she'd stop Moses. She would stop me; she'd stop anybody! I'm such an antihero it never once occurred to me that *I* might have walked up quietly behind him and "successfully" taken the gun.

Something inside a wall was scratching hard at wood. It made goose bumps ripple across my flesh.

Moses held the open ends of the shotgun to Gal's temple. I was an angle-witness, moved—and yet I felt and understood his every move. At least I suspected a thin correlation.

Her eyes looking straight up
into his
and he was again either talking to himself or to her. His foot, its pressure, made it difficult for her to breathe.
Now.
One blast

BLAM

now, silence   . and the smoke, lazy, drifting up from the barrel. Between his legs, the nose of the weapon, dangling.

There was a sudden loss of sensation in my left hand. My only good hand, really. And my left eye began to throb, to jump; spasms. What   was swelling and wouldn't stop until it reached a certain point at which it would bust   ? I became quietly more frantic as the pressure choked me. And I was frozen.

A heart attack?

As I stepped into the room, like an animal blindly going to slaughter, behind me I heard the strain of human gagging and the sudden surge of vomiting.

Now, Moses comes alive again. He lifts his weapon and points it briefly in the direction of the screaming kids huddled together on the other side of the window. And I can't imagine why they remain there like that, facing his madness.

It's all too much like a nightmare. I want to wake up and yet I know only too well, there's nothing to wake up to. Except, of course, a more intense perception of *this*.

At that moment a powerful hand gripped my shoulder and slammed me to the side, against a woman who'd suddenly come to my side. The poor woman hit the wall with a dull thud and screamed, a sharp, loud, singular, and nerve-wracking cry.

Moses wheeled around as though he expected to see Veronica's ghost coming to haunt him. Wet streaks ran down his swollen cheeks and he sniffed his nose. His dark face emitted a very subjective and self-righteous look. He dropped his left hand and wiped a blazing tear from his puffy right eye.

Moses stood facing me. The strong hand still held me by the shoulder and a voice behind me spoke to Moses. Lookit, fella, the voice said, you don't want to do this awful thing . . . Why don't you give me the gun, huh . . . ?

The tip of the Winchester was still smoking.

Come here Moses, Moses Westby said to me.

I tried to pull away, to go to him. The hand took a tighter hold on me. I tried to turn around to see who was holding me; but I couldn't—the pressure of the hand was quite rigid. There was something protective yet deeply annoying in it.

I said come here, Moses repeated.

Again I tried and again I couldn't free myself.

I felt a chill that would never thaw; my knees began to buckle, but I refused to fall. There was a ringing in my ears from the shotgun blasts and the monster in me continued to swell— near the breaking point. My eyes were burning as the smoke drifted up.

LORD HAVE MERCY! somebody behind me screamed.

Moses was aiming the gun at me. I looked straight into the eye squinted over the shotgun.

He pulled the trigger　　　　　BLAM
　　　the blast filled my ears
I felt it
　　　but I continued to watch him. He turned the Winchester around and adjusted the barrel inside his mouth then, quickly he pulled the trigger　　　　　BLAM

And even long after the ringing in my ears was quieter there was still the pounding of voices and feet shuffling against my senses and things, possibly hands, jumping and fumbling at the nape of my neck. My predicament seemed so morbid, lonely, inaccessible. I was startled by a painful lack of reality. I hadn't been able to believe my eyes and I still couldn't accept my wound, my own blood, my death.

　　　I'd seen his skull scatter. The chips and pieces, the slime, fly- ing up to the ceiling, spreading high up the side of the wall, and instantly dripping down in slow lazy drops. It was too much.

It was a long time before I slept but when I did in my sleep I saw Moses Westby wet his finger, hold up his arm, and hav- ing nothing to make an impression on, in the air, he drew

murmured something; then dropped softly and quietly like a boneless creature falling in a silent film.

To me, in any case, it was clearly impossible to stay where I was so I found myself drifting and searching for a place, any place in which I might feel a certain degree of comfort. I moved northeast slowly, it possibly took years. Also, while all this physical activity was taking place, who and what I am was also in flux; anyway, it was around this time that I began to consciously feel that I was at last on the road to self-determination.

Also, if I were living more consciously than unconsciously I wanted to come to fully understand that middle land between the two as well as the other two. But what I truly suspected was I somehow was suspended in a kind of pivot between the two, conscious and unconscious. I felt like a creature unable to sleep *and,* at the same time, unable to wake.

But I felt that I could expect my life to create its own terms. I suppose simply because that was what had been happening all along but the difference now might be that I would be in a new context. I was hopeful anyway. I was not unaware, however, that I'd brought along with me, my old schemes, my fears, my limitations, my social habits, when I hardly needed them, and furthermore, I'd left some of myself behind.

Anyway, I've come to this new city called New York. I haven't been in New York two weeks when I luck up on this crazy unreal job analyzing and coding and classifying newspaper reportage of urban riot incidents. They call me a research analyst and my focus is on riot incidents from the preceding year. I work in an office crammed with pretty sexy girls in a building on a street that is broad, called Broadway; and I have to work (no, I don't really *have* to work!) shifty hours sometimes so wacky they seem to go counterclockwise.

143

At first, naturally, it is all very strange: I can hardly believe I won't ever again have to confront Slick nor Thursday nor Lucy Nasteylipp. They seem so much a part of the past they are now almost unreal. And I've changed my name slightly: sometimes I think of myself as Moses Eastby.

And, though there was the fast feeling of having jumped from one place to another, along with it was a hard sense of having moved *back* in time. I'd always suspected I was extremely old; now, suddenly, for the first time, I felt quite young—I was a young man. And I *felt* like a young man. And what did it matter that I still possessed a lot of senile or childish habits?

One of the first incidents to stagger me took place one night as opposed to one day.

I lived on the Lower East Side and I was on my way home from seeing the movie, *I Am Curious (Yellow)*. I came up out of the frosty mouth of the subway at 14th Street and 1st Avenue. It was a weekday, late, and there were hardly any people on the street. Walking, my mind usually does it own thing and this time was no exception. I was trying to remember what all of them looked like, those people I'd left behind, but I couldn't remember a single face. Not only that, many of the names had escaped me.

I'd just turned off 14th Street where wet traffic lights and automobile noise splashed through the lazy snow-night. And I glanced over my shoulder because I either saw or felt someone following me.

Yes. Someone was. And I thought she was a sad little old man bundled up in the night. There was my own snow-crunching footfalls as I plodded along. Or maybe it was just my imagination. Many people came this way: the person behind me didn't necessarily have to be following me. *But she was.*

And just when I thought I'd come to live without clog or bruise of curse. In a sort of technological safety. Again and again, it was being shown to me: there would never be safety. The cumbering shadowy figure behind me was one example of the living proof.

The voice is definitely that of a woman and it is strangely familiar. I'm clogged suddenly with concern.

I think, of course, she's panhandling and will hit on me for a couple of pennies or a nickel. It is what one comes to expect on the streets of the Lower East Side.

Just as sharp as the voice a piece of metal is introduced to my spine. I know it isn't anything designed to heat up strangers freezing like Bowery beggars on brisk snow-packed sidewalks. It spoke obviously out of another character. *But a woman pulling a stickup?* Well. Perhaps in New York at least the Woman's Liberation Movement had begun to succeed.

But that voice! I know that voice! as she snaps, *Get inside that doorway*—MOVE!

My irritation is strangely indulged by my curiosity. This might be a *real* Location Shooting for all I know.

So, into this colorless dreary building I scamper. There isn't the slightest twitch of female falaciousness in her. And she's so bundled up I can't yet see her face. Aside from killing me, what can she do worse than rape or rob? Well. Liberated women have the right to do anything men do. No question about it. But that is something that gets slowly through my head.
Yet, to have a woman force me into a hump in a shabby hallway in a gritty city   ? Her morbid appearance in no way helped toward comfort.

Also.

Part of the irritation I felt (I think) was due to having to *now* deal with, without being able to come to terms with, an existential moment less crucial, less absolute than an ultimate act. Well. I simply didn't believe she was going to kill me. And I wondered briefly: could there be a condition outside death to which I'd entrust the destruction of my "sense of self" without concession or restraint willingly or unwillingly in the interest of some "idea" or "cause." It *was* the proper moment for such reflection.

We stand at the bottom of what appears to be the steepest emptiest stairway to closed and bolted and silent rooms I have ever encountered.

Her back is to the streetlight but   I   think
I   know   who   she   is   .She
can't be! No! It's impossible!   How did Nasteylipp get to
New York and how'd she turn so old so quickly   ?   O
fuck this must be a dream!

Nasteylipp?

Shut up, the woman said. I got something to show you!

She whipped open her huge black coat and revealed her
shrunken naked body. My eyes focused on her sad furry triangle. A sprinkling of gray hairs decorated it.

And in this unclear and crucial moment I dared to look beyond her to the street—for some smoothly hidden reason. With
white paint, in the middle of the street somebody had written
in large letters

FUCK EVERYBODY

That message hadn't been there this morning, but now, there
it was and here I was, sure, absolutely sure I was facing none
other than Queen Nasteylipp herself. A sloppy thought: My,
how time flies!

(It's simply the *way* we move through the world.)

What happened to the red paint?

What?

Your cunt, it used to be red—remember . . . ?

Who are you? Nasteylipp asked, squinting her eyes in the
shadows.

Moses.

The little skinny jerk who used to live—no! Don't tell me!
It can't be!

She slapped herself on the forehead. At the same time the
heavy coat fell back over her nakedness.

She took me by the shoulders and turned me so that the
light got to more of my face.

You really are Moses aren't you. Well! I'll be damned!

146

Small world, huh.

You're fucking right, kid. You've changed a lot, boy. Have *I* changed? she asked.

I tried to see her in a better light but I couldn't.

Well, I said, your cunt ain't red no more.

I shaved it off. I never understood why that squirrely pair of coons pulled that trick on me no-how.

I'm sure it *meant* something. They weren't just playing around.

And cutting that boy's dick off like that. I *heard* about it. Say! she snapped, you heard about B.B., didn't you   ?

No.

He got married. Has children—three of 'em. All girls. Pretty things, too. He drinks beer and watches TV. He's a typesetter these days.

No lie?

And you know about Grew, I guess.

No, I don't.

Didn't you *hear?* He killed himself!

What?

Yes. Jumped in that ol' canyon where the Indians used to do it.

A moment of silence.

Tell me something Lucy.

What?

Is that a real gun and what were you planning to do to me?

Well. You see I got this thing about exposing my body, see. It gives me a real charge. I like to force a man at gunpoint to *look* at it and dare him to touch. I've got to get even with you men some kinda way, *shit.*

O was she funny!

147

I wondered how she'd look if I struck a match to her shabby coat and watch her swoop up in liquid cracking snapping flames like one of those martyrs in the name of Buddha video-taped in Vietnam. How would she feel sizzling like Sunday morning breakfast smoked bacon? Actually if she were only an invention of my mind no matter how pernicious my sadism such a death had too much style for her.

Listen, I said to Nasteylipp, I don't live far from here.
Would you like to come up for coffee or a drink?

She looked a little embarrassed. I could see her better now and I liked her less. She opened her mouth to speak but no words came.

I said, If you have something else to do . . .

As a matter of fact, I *do* have something to do. Maybe another time.

As she spoke she was backing out the hallway.

Really. It's a fact that all New Yorkers are from out of town. Therefore it really isn't so terribly unusual in New York to run into people you've known, say, in a place like Chickamauga. After all, who would want to stay forever in Chickamauga?

Of all the people I met in New York perhaps the most surprising was my wife, Oni Dunn.

We'd been sitting and talking together for over two hours before I recognized her. But it took her even longer: I had to refresh her memory.

Oni was different now: she was plush, pretty, and sexy. She looked tastier than a chocolate chip cookie! For the first time I noticed she had freckles and a pretty, turned-up nose. She was wearing a green leather mini dress and black sandals.

And she was more cheerful than before. Or maybe her wisecracks about herself were designed to conceal misery. In any case, she was now always smiling, giggling, or laughing. But nervously.

We were into the afternoon in a 2nd Avenue bar on the Lower East Side. I was tossing around in its glass a double shot of straight burnt orange (the color) liquor. Oni was nibbling at a tall damp glass of Comfort Collins.

So you're an actress now, huh?

That's right Moses. But I still have a *lot* to learn. I have this very nice director friend of mine who's very helpful—so I feel like I'm making progress.

You certainly have come a long way from Chickamauga.

I don't even tell people I was born there.

> Her laughter was delicious. I wanted to grab her and sink my teeth into her plump lips.

Does it bother you *now* that you know who I am?

> No. Why should it? said Oni.

Oh, I don't know . . . Maybe you'd like to forget Chickamauga and everybody from that part of the world.

> Oh, seeing *you*, Moses, doesn't bother me. You're not like you used to be anyway.

How's that?

> You know—skerry and shy.

Her giggling infected me. We sat there giggling together; then, I finished my drink and started eyeing the shapely female rumps perched on the barstools. I didn't know what else to say to her, since my mind was on fucking her, and I *still* couldn't say *that* to her.

———◆———

Oni stands naked beside my bed. The tips of my fingers trace invisible lines on her smooth, shapely thigh, down to her leg as far as I can reach. She looks very happy, delicious, and bright. And she smells very fresh even excessively clean. A smile begins to break at the edges of her face and she touches the top of my woolly head.

Her naked right knee came onto the orange quilt blanket and her face was menacing, but playfully so. Then she's suddenly struck as she's been struck so many times in the past, by a painting on the wall behind the bed. It depicts a cut-up orange nude against a deep green background. The artist might have called it "The Confused Lady." Now, turns her attention back to me and gives a warning: I'm going to eat you up, to savor every morsel of your tender and plump hocks and especially your gristle.

Her aggressiveness made me feel a little unmanly. But I held tight. One has to see.

She tried to come on like a grizzly but I grabbed the spongy parts of her and threw her down and locked her down with my legs crossed under and over her waist. She gave me a little playful scream; meanwhile, opening her thighs and kicking at but missing me.

You can't have me, I said firmly.

I'll have you by the balls, Mister! she shouted. And she struggled.

When I was tired I relaxed and she got on her knees and holding my rod close to her mouth, pretended she was speaking into a microphone.

Testing one two three testing one two three can you hear me
can you hear me this is a test I say this is a test ladies and
gentlemen this is a test over—

Then, she giggled.

What a sweet giggle! I said, Every time I see you, baby, you
look better!

It's just the buzz you've got, Oni said, resting on her elbows
and ass. But thank you, anyway.

Suddenly, I felt her teeth sink into my flesh.

Ouch! that's good!

Already I felt the fun of having her here as opposed to having
her in her dreary apartment. I always did like my own bed
best.

I tried to get away but she tightened her grip; her hot tight
naked skin brushing swishy against mine, creating new circuits.

She giggled and said, You're acting like *the* woman.

It's cause I have something to fear.

I felt the sudden stab of her wet tongue slide around in my
ear and when I rolled over I felt that same tongue sliding
powerfully up the inside of my left thigh. She gripped my
organ with her hands and held on like a sailor pulling the
lifts of a mast. I closed my eyes and saw the quick flash of a
Gaff ketch sailing smoothly across the horizon. My mind wan-
ders. And there were so many questions I wanted to ask her
but they could certainly wait. I, too, could wait. And certainly
her answers, if they ever came, would have to wait. And yet it
was still true that what I'd been waiting to see and feel would
never become a reality.

Many of my long-felt desires had been fulfilled but there was
so much yet to be done. I had a kitchen cabinet full of tooth-
picks and packed away neatly in a suitcase I had those candy
wrappers the soldiers had thrown to us. But my objectives were
changing. Moses had committed murder but he hadn't killed
the people I considered my enemies. I still dreamed of freedom
and though I was now, in New York, free of that terribly re-

stricted penal area, Chickamauga, the freedom *I* dreamed of still eluded me.

> Oni's tongue worked around my kneecap. Then, she began sucking my fingers, one at a time. I let my mind drift in circles, following her motion.

I let her play a moment longer then, pulled her up so that her mouth was even with my own and, into hers I spoke.

> Do you remember Nasteylipp?

You mean Lucy?

> Right.

Yes; what about her?

> Nothing, really, I said, suddenly deciding not to tell Oni about the incident.

You're very strange, Oni said. You know, John, her husband, tried to rape me once.

> I groaned and quickly kissed her, to stop the flow of words. Poor words, sad words. The kiss was long, wet, easy, and good. Without strain.

A voice from the TV said, Cheap thrills!

> I rolled Oni over and lay on top of her, without breaking the kiss.

She was murmuring, asking me something, and I, without understanding her, said, Yes, I feel it.

> Her hair, parted down the middle, fell forward over her face, as she tried to turn away from me, in—?—confusion. I could see us in the mirror, her copper-colored face and chest and hands and arms, her closed straining eyes, black slits, her large impressive Afro hairdo, like a crown, against the zinc and Chinese and titanium whites and pale yellows and naples yellows and pinks of the bedspread and sheets and pillow cases.

Baby, I said, you are really good to *look* at!

> Is that *all?*

Her fingers now skipped slowly up and down the jumpy surface of the skin under my arms. And I wanted to see her sway under the impact of my battering—*if* she would give me a chance! The tips of her fingers crawled up my spine, and I could hardly swat the flyspeck-"size" thought that there was somebody in the closet listening to and watching us through the keyhole. And I felt guilty for thinking that. I also felt *crazy* for thinking it because, for one reason among a number of others, the person I suspected of being there was Veronica. But since that was impossible I let my mind begin asking itself a certain type of question: like, why did I need to play this game and *why* with Veronica; would I never be free of her; should I ever be?

I finally entered Oni and we began moving together at a slow, quiet pace.

Soon, I rolled off and without breaking the circuit, we continued, facing each other, on our sides. The flesh of her ass twitched and wiggled under my hands. Her large spongy breasts bounced against my cheeks. She was clinging insistently and the electric suction occupied us completely. And from my angle I can still see us in the mirror. We are overcast with the afternoon's green filmy tint. The cheeks of her ass are very beautiful in their rhythm.

The closet door is slightly ajar. It offers nothing but shadows, not secrets, not strangers, not old friends, nor Veronica. I have to force my eyes away from it. Keep them focused on the mirror. Yes, watch Oni's rump.

Why, she whispered, have we waited all this time to have our wedding night?

Because, Oni, before now it would have been a farce.

She giggled. Well, it still seems a little ridiculous.

Immediately, I felt my penis begin shrinking inside her. Why did she have to say such a dumb thing?

Besides, I said, we've done it in *your* bed a lot—Why weren't those times the honeymoon?

I said wedding night, *not* honeymoon.

154

Let's forget it, shall we.

We screwed in silence for awhile before she spoke again.

You know, you may not believe nor understand this, but I think the whole world is moving backwards in time. I really believe that. You know, she said, I've been reading Einstein.

Oh, really.

Yes, I have. It's very complicated.

I pulled out. I said, Turn on your stomach.

What?

On your stomach.

Why?

Just turn on your stomach. You'll see why.

She giggled. You mean I'll *feel* why.

She rolled over with a groan.

For several moments I sat there running my fingers along her thighs.

Stop teasing me. I want to feel you inside me, Oni said.

I got on her and entered her again.

Is it good to you, Oni?

You know it is. Oh OH! A H! But that hurts when you do it like that. Go easy.

Yes dear.

She tried to turn around to see the expression on my face but she couldn't make it. She sighed and relaxed her head on her folded arms. The face of her watch was looking at me as I moved back and forth on her thighs.

For a while I watched our bodies in the mirror. Still, I felt a very long way from an orgasm. It was like my heart wasn't truly in it. But I watched my rod slide in and out of her.

Then quite suddenly she lifted herself on her elbows but didn't try to look back to see me as she spoke.

Moses, she said, *what* in the fuck are you doing?

What'd you mean, Oni?

She hissed before speaking.

You know damn well you don't want to make love! So why don't you STOP PLAYING AROUND   ?

I couldn't decide right away how her words left me feeling, except I knew the impact wasn't spelled g-o-o-d.

I got off and sat with my back against the wall and she joined me. We both were looking at her, *from* the mirror.

While Oni dressed I watched her. Halfway dressed, she did a few fancy ballet steps before the mirror. Obviously remembering the body skills she'd mastered in her New York drama school.

Though I'd had something of an orgasm I felt vaguely cheated but it was not a new feeling, in New York, nor anywhere. I dropped the heavy lids of my eyes.

For some reason I spoke before I knew what I was saying. I said, You know, it was Matilda who I wanted all along.

Who? What?

Matilda. The girl in the ice box with the butterfly coming out of her cunt.

You must be half asleep, Moses, talking like that.

No, Oni, Matilda was very real. She used to swing herself in her swing on her porch in the dark.

I think we need to go away, take a vacation, she said.

Yes, *yeah!* I said, getting excited. To another country! We have enough money for the first time in our lives!

While Oni was in the shower I lay there thinking, because I couldn't help myself, about Moses and Veronica. Funny, they were the first people i knew and I'd probably never completely stop thinking of them. And now that I'd lost them forever I'd probably (though I hoped not) think about them even more! Yet, even while knowing it was pointless. What I had to do really well, even if I thought at times that I'd already done it, was try to make peace with each of them, in my mind. Learn to live with my sense of them and with the *self* they, in their ways, had given me. It would certainly improve my relationship with Oni, if that were possible.

I didn't want to just go on and on without trying to understand the past. Some of it was beginning to make sense but a lot of it was still dim. Like the incident with Moses: I'd let him see my loose tooth if he'd promise not to try to pull it and the first thing he did when my mouth fell open was to snatch it out and say, See, that wasn't so bad, was it. And Slick holding me upsidedown over the suicide canyon—or was it a dream. The echoes of my screams rippling through the forest. And B.B. and Grew throwing me in the creek when they knew I couldn't swim. Just to see me go crazy with fear. And what I thought about while watching animals or fowl mate. And my worship of cowboys. And being forced in the first grade to learn how to skip: A girl would take me out into the playground each afternoon and try to teach me how. It took some time but I mastered it though without wanting to. And how they all laughed at me when I shouted I saw a ball of fire falling from the night sky. And the beating I got for secretly keeping a stray dog under the house. I woke up with the belt coming against my head, cutting through my sleep-stung eyes. And the beating I got because my prick got hard while Thursday was giving me a bath. And the time Gal had been left as my ward and I lost her and was so panic-stricken I lost my voice and even the ability to walk. My furious and morbid love for colored stones frogs moles lizards vampires and the forest itself. And highways, always highways. And the frustration I felt when the free white citizens forced an old couple in their eighties to fuck so they (the whites) could see two old black people doing it. And how I worried about the size of my meat. And my wet dreams. And the time Grady attempted to throw himself into the fireplace into the flames—without success, though he did burn the tail end of his nightgown. And all the mysterious hours in the woods setting rabbit traps trying to catch rabbits. And the teacher, that time, who had a heart attack in front of the classroom—watching them carry her out, wondering about life and death. And being called a fucking nigger by a drunk white man. Being told I couldn't drink from an all-white water fountain. And the afternoon I spent watching buzzards devour the carcass of a dead cow. And my horror of dirty hands—especially my own. And dreams, trapped in coffins, unable to move or falling, falling, falling, endlessly falling. Or one leg missing and trying to walk on the one that remains. And watching Karo trying to suck his own peter. And feeling always the distance between myself and every or anybody. And the taste of cabbage that smell of piss and dead birds with their stomachs ripped out. B.B.'s big prick; Grew, castrated. How does he pee? And I want to escape—do I shoot them to be free?

> I know there is a haunting quality in all this. Also, I know this confession does not relieve me and that I did not, by leaving the worst area of the prison, transcend it—not yet. No matter *how* free *I feel* I have yet to *be* free!

One thing: if Moses had a horrifying life, it was also filled with beauty. And if I am anybody   I am   Moses.

It made me feel like a renewed person. Being with the Puerto Rican girl, I mean. When I met her she was wearing a fishnet dress, red panties, sandals, and that is all. Actually, she wasn't wearing the sandals, she was carrying them in her hand.

A creamy chocolate complexion. She was standing on the stairway, the muddy yellow lights of our dingy hallway turned her large, lusty black eyes purple.

When she sees me coming up or going down she looks at me with the hunger you might expect to witness in the eye of a middle-aged woman: that serious, unblinking, gut-felt hunger! Stubborn, begging eyes. I'd seen her many times before we talked and I knew the face. Clearly. The lust in it. And it was rare in a Puerto Rican girl; but she was stretching out on a new wavelength. And I kid you not: *I* wanted to stretch out *on her;* try her air intake, her crank shaft, her fuel pump, her combustion chamber, pistons, cylinders, and valve. Take a ride *in* her. And she looked imminently ready!

I gave her the kind of smile that certainly told her what was on my mind. She shook a playful finger at me blushing. I liked the way her nose wrinkled when she smiled.

But there were two questions behind the smooth surface of my eyes that I couldn't answer yet nor make peace with: what does she mean to me and what would making love with her prove? I came to this: do I seek to free myself from some aspect of the prison of the self, through her?

She follows me up the stairway, playing on the steps as she climbs. She snaps like a pup at my pants leg. I begin playing with a notion. It at once hits out of and into me as taboo but the assault of temptation is too crucial to be dismissed lightly.

How can I run and hide from something that's in me? The
hallway, as always, smells of fresh piss—both dog and human.
Warm waves slapping inside my intentions. Is it possible to
pull the stem of this new thing? Inner streams of my own pity
feeding the poverty of my present moment, this ache—the
danger of it!

Suddenly   her mother   a woman as hard and
     as big   as a washtub   rushes up   to
me and   plunges   a 95¢ butcher knife   into
     an area   of my   throat   :I
stab this fear   and   stack it   under
     the flower bed   rocks
of some safety   valve

I shiver to fornicate (though I don't like that word) with this
precious angel, this Hispanic nymphet! To fuck her in the
lotus posture, to rock her till her rectal axis and spinal cord
break with love!

With a nod of my head I consent for her to follow me.

Also, it occurs to me that Oni might right in the high heat of
this love make use of her key to my apartment; but that's too
much like fiction. She would *never* come in on me like that. Anyway, from a moral point of view, I do not believe in being sexually unfaithful *when* I am in love—but I am not there. Right?
Then, so what if she comes in. You don't ever have to answer
such questions. What you have often depends on what you dig.
And what you dig is no surprise. Ever.

I am carrying a bag containing food items; she comes in,
quietly, looking suspicious and fearful and behind us, I lock
the door and place my bag on the kitchen table. The kitchen
is the first room you enter. Where you come from matters too.

Together we go into the front where the light is better. I fall
on the couch and yawn but she waits awkwardly; her pink
tongue, in quick lizardlike movements, licks the corky dark
ridges of her chapped lips.

What's your name, baby?

She grins and twists her fingers together. Cross her legs.

Huh?

161

Josefina.

Josefina. *Ah!*

Do you have any money you can give me?

Josefina, come sit beside me.

She did as she was asked.

Now, tell me, why do you want money?

She was blushing but she looked directly into my eyes.

Why do *you* yourself need money, huh?

I hate the idea of money, I said. Not really sure of what I meant exactly. But feeling something like that.

Then give it to me, all your money, give it to me, if you hate it.

Without a moment's hesitation I took out my wallet and gave her the thirty-five or so dollars in it. But Josefina gave me a puzzled look. She chuckled.

You're crazy, she said.

Maybe. Yes.

She watched my eyes as her right hand moved slowly toward the paper currency and, at the same time, she was on the verge of laughter. Her dimples were forming.

It's not a game, Josefina. The money is yours.

In other words then I can have this—right?

It's yours. I'm giving it to you.

But what'd I have to do for you in return, y'know . . .

Nothing. Do nothing for me.

She gave me a disbelieving look that was more than a little frustrating because I really meant what I was doing and saying.

You have nice nipples.

She tucked in her chin and tried to see them.

I like—how do you say?—freedom, you know? You know what I mean . . . I like to feel free, so I wear just this.

You look very good.

Ah! I know what's on *your* mind! Your name—what's your name?

Moses.

Like in the Bible?

No, not quite. But something like that.

Meanwhile she folded the money tightly in her hand.

Say, you know, if you want some grass, I can sell you some grass. You *do* smoke, right? I mean, you know, like you already give me money, so I give you a little present too, I give you some good grass. Okay?

No thank you. You don't have to give me anything. I wanted to give you the money for nothing. No reason.

She scratched her head and frowned while watching me. The hand that held the money was sweating and she cleared her throat against the silence.

Don't you play no music, don't you have no radio or something?

Yes, it's in the kitchen, on the refrigerator. Turn it on, if you like.

Yes, I like. I like music. It makes me feel free, you know.

I know.

She came back from the kitchen and the apartment was filled with loud Spanish music.

Say! Moses, you got ears for Eddie Palmieri and Ray Barretto?

I assumed she was referring to the musicmakers of the sounds coming from the radio. I dug it. The drums. The Latin beat.

Yes.

I got a sister, her name is Angela; she don't like no music, man. She stops up her ears everytime the radio is on. She go like this—

And Josefina demonstrates.

163

Suddenly, I burst out laughing. I am happy, unexpectedly so.

She is standing before me.

Can you dance, Moses?

No.

You *can* dance but you don't want to dance—right?

Wrong. I can't dance. But I'd like to watch you.

And she'd already started moving her hips. She was apparently holding hands with an imaginary partner as she got into some quick short steps. She held her bottom lip pressed furiously under her top teeth, as she moved about. Suddenly, she looked sharply at me, obviously was embarrassed, laughed at herself, then fell on the couch beside me.

Through the music I heard loud knocking at the door.

Ah shit! cried Josefina, and jumped up and ran toward the window.

Where're you going?

If that's my father he'll kill me. Unlock this thing and let me go down the fire escape!

For a moment I was tempted to argue with her while the knocking continued at the door.

I found the key on my chain that unlocks the lock to the window gate, pulled it back, pushed up the window, and watched her scurrying out and down and away.

When I got to the door no one was there. So, I closed it, turned off the radio; then stood before the mirror and in carefully examining my penis discovered nothing new about it.

I was speaking to Oni.

I want the chance to shape my own future; to be able to make decisions in reference to what I will or will not do. I want to have some say in the programming of my own day-to-day existence.

But Oni wasn't listening. Perhaps she was right not to listen. Maybe I said nothing worth attention. Or something too remote.

We were sitting in my bed after a long sweaty fuck and vaguely watching TV.

I turned to her.

What do you want?

I don't know. I don't even know *who* I am; I don't even have an image of myself. I mean, I can't imagine *what* I look like to other people.

Do you feel free, Oni?

Yeah, I guess so. I mean, you know, *how* free can we be?

She now sounded wise and I was ashamed of having thought of her as a giggling foolish woman. Girl, rather.

You know, Moses, you're a very serious-minded person. I think you should check yourself. I mean, what good does it do to walk around serious all the time? I remember Moses Westby, he wasn't all that serious all the time. He used to laugh and joke with kids and he was fun. How come you can't be fun, too?

I don't know.

You should try it. It really isn't hard, you know.

But *how* should I start?

> Just laugh and relax sometime. I bet you even walk around holding the muscles in your asshole tight, don't you.

Oni suddenly ran her hand beneath my balls and tried to insert a finger into my anus. I jumped and moved away.

> See, see what I mean. You're just not playful. You should get outside, more, too. Buy a bike and go riding. Go swimming. You know? Do things. Just kinda let it all hang out, be free.

I *want* to but I don't know if riding a bike and swimming will be the means to freedom.

> Try it. How do you know unless you try it?

Yeah.

> You say *yeah* very cynically.

I just said, Yeah. I wasn't trying to be cynical.

> But you sound cynical, like you don't believe anything is going to work. I mean, if you start with that attitude, *nothing* will work.

All right, all right.

> Now you're mad.

I'm not!

> Oni sighed. I guess I have no right to say any of this to you, really. Maybe you're happy with the way you are. Are you?

I don't dislike myself but there's room for improvement.

> Uh-huh, room for improvement. Did you know that you're really a dull person, Moses?

What'd you mean?

> Just what I said. Dull dull dull. *I mean it!* You really are, man! And if I'd known in the beginning I don't think I'd have ever gotten involved with you. But don't take it personally. It's for your own good. It's not something hopeless; it's something you can work on. You don't have to be the way you are. And don't think I'm trying to *re*make you either. I can't do that if I wanted to.

166

But do you want to remake me?

I just said I *don't,* didn't I!

Well, Oni, I said, feeling hurt, we can't all be as exciting as you are! You know we can't all have charisma!

It's not a matter of charisma. But you're being cynical. I can see that. And you're taking what I'm saying all wrong. Lest you can take advice, Moses, you're never going to improve yourself. And another thing—no, maybe I shouldn't bring it up.

Go ahead, bring it up!

She was silent for a moment as she watched the TV screen. Beneath the cover I gently held my rod, waiting. I was trying to reduce the hardness of the texture of the defense mechanism in me that now was building against her speech. I wanted to hear even bad advice. To learn how to see it and to get from it what was useful.

I've wanted to bring this up before but—well, it's a touchy subject.

There shouldn't be anything we can't talk about, Oni.

You're right.

But she said nothing else for a moment.

How do you *feel* about sex, Moses?

What'd you mean?

Do you enjoy it?

Yes.

Always?

Most of the time.

What about the times when you don't enjoy it. When are those times?

There was a long silence.

Don't you know?

I couldn't give Oni an answer.

167

Well, she said, the reason I brought it up is: *you don't satisfy me sexually.* And I can feel something in you that's being held back. Do you understand what I'm trying to say?

Not quite.

It's like a little while ago, when you were on top. Remember?

Of course I remember.

Well. I just didn't feel *any*thing! I got the feeling that your *heart* wasn't in it. I never feel *warmth* generated from you when we're screwing. It's always so cold. And you always finish before I have a chance to come. I mean, I HAVE NEVER HAD AN ORGASM WITH YOU.

Maybe you *can't* have one.

That's not true! I *know* I can have an orgasm. I've had many orgasms—many! many!

I felt crushed, completely. But I felt she was telling the truth because often I'd felt *her* holding back during the act. I sensed she was many times more sexually potent and even physically stronger than I would ever be. But with whom had she had so many fucking orgasms?

Oni was nervously lighting a cigarette.

I hope you can *take* all this, she said.

I can take it.

With her free hand gently she touched my arm.

Moses, could it be *because* of Veronica—I mean, that you can't *feel* it . . .

But I do—I do feel it!

Then, how come *I* can't feel you feeling it?

Oni, I honestly don't know.

Do you know, I've made love with about three hundred guys. And usually *I* have an orgasm. I never told you, but I made it once with Moses Westby, when I was very little. He was one of the first. It happened in the woods, in the back seat of his Cadillac. He put me through ten orgasms in less than two hours.

168

And I'm not saying this to try to make you feel bad or anything. It's just that when we fuck I don't feel you. And the only reason I've stayed with you as long as I have is, I keep hoping things will improve. But now, I'm beginning to doubt.

> On the word "doubt" her voice dropped and other than the mechanical babble from the TV there was quiet.

Did you ever make it with B.B.?

> Yes, Moses. Several times. With him, too, I had an orgasm every time. And with Grew, too. Grew was especially good. I mean we really had great sexual communication.

Sex is very important to you, isn't it, Oni?

> My voice sounded defensive as hell. Even angry.

It's no more important than it should be.

> I felt so crushed that my hand under the cover stopped playing with my meat.

She mashed out her cigarette in the ashtray on her lap and placed the tray on the bookshelf beside the bed. She took a deep breath and let it out.

> I knew I shouldn't have brought up any of this.

I'm glad you did, Oni.

> I wonder . . .

I'd sensed that some of this was true, anyway, Oni; and isn't it better that it's out in the open   ?

> *I* think so—and I hope you do, too.

I felt cold, very cold. I wanted to be alone with my defeat. I didn't have the heart nor the nerve to ask her to leave so I got up.

> Where're you going?

For a walk.

> Oh, man, she said, why'd I have to open my mouth!

Listen! *Stop* apologizing! I'm *glad* you did!

> And she lay there watching me dress.

So, this was part of the lowdown, the real dirt and nittygritty juice, on what becoming an escapee was leading to.

Part of the definition of an escapee is that he attains the curious status of adulthood. It may not really mean anything in terms of true liberation but the escapee is nevertheless stuck with not just the condition but also the stigma.

An escapee does not come to know anymore about the Beginning than those strictly confined in one of the more terrible penal areas. An escapee who does not know his real name neither necessarily learns it nor makes more peace with the one that has stuck to him.

But don't misunderstand: I was not yet outside the penal system. There was left plenty of mental ground to get beyond. To say nothing of the physical area.

And in my dreams it happened over and over that I was marched before a firing squad. And always, just before the firing started, I was snatched away to safety by strong hands belonging to someone I don't know and therefore can't name. In a way it was as annoying as *coitus interruptus*. And probably has created in me just as many psychological and emotional problems as withdrawal might in somebody who practices it.

And all the while, no matter what happens, my mind goes back to the beginning. Not the real Beginning, which we can never go back to in any real sense, but to the beginning of my own memory. I'm not referring to what I've been told. No matter how true or untrue any of it is, I am shuffling and weighing the facts and artifacts of those ruins that have been recorded in my own sensibility.

There were so many things I saw and heard that I not once clearly nor fully understood. Like John Flower being a tax collector. What did it mean? He certainly wasn't a real tax collector! Or Gal turning from a dance instructor into a spy.

Nobody treated me as though I deserved an explanation. I suddenly discovered myself *alive* and the horror of one day no longer being alive put me in a sort of cool state of permanent shock. I walked around looking at everybody as though they couldn't possibly be *real!*

And that distant war. The soldiers. The army trucks. The candy wrappers. Wasn't it all something I read in a comic book?

How did I survive this long? How do I go on living?

You ready?

Yes.

We took a taxi to the airport; our tickets and passports were checked; we moved in the herd onto the jet, to tourist seats in the back. The aircraft taxied out to the runway. This would be Oni's first flight out of the country. Either I had once before left the country in actuality or in a long, sweet dream. In any case, I remember once being away for a long time.

We were high up now. I had the seat by the window. Oni turned to me and said, What am I doing here with you? Where are we going   ?

We landed in a very warm but cool Latin country where the people were, in color, like me, a rich tan complexion; and they spoke their own brand of Spanish. Oni, who had Spanish in high school, was understood by them when she spoke. However, when they spoke, the same was not true. So, we went about making ourselves understood though without understanding.

I grew a beard and cultivated a deeper silence. Quiet, I was happy; the beard made me feel better.

But Oni   ?   Why was I holding on to her, was it just habit   , fear   of being   alone?

It was clear, in any case, she had become very dependent on me. Sure, she was frustrated, but she felt very *safe* with me. There was something very fatherly and protective in my personality.

Yes. I wanted her to need me but not too much. I also wanted her to be strong enough to be her own person. Her dependency frightened me because it was too stifling to me and to her it was immobilizing.   I knew all this before we went away together and yet I had not the power to do anything about it. I, too, was terribly dependent on her.

She looked back a couple of times to see (I suppose) if I were following her. She was wearing her new Spanish style dark-blue dress with a wild high waist and narrow slim sleeves and with a turkey-feather styled rayon velvet collar and cuffs altered so that it hung only half way down her large gleaming golden thighs.

Oni has a sexy way of walking.

Catcalls and romantic whistling from the local men. I followed her along Juarez, where she was vaguely window-shopping, and continued to follow her up the malecon. It was very pleasant along the bay; the wind was coming in from the ocean and, at this time of the afternoon, the tourists were mostly the ones out. Two hours ago, at one o'clock most of the shops had closed down and wouldn't open again till four.   I felt deep shame; but I knew even then, the real reason I followed her: I wanted *evidence*. I had already convicted her in my mind and now I wanted proof of her infidelity. Of course, that infidelity didn't exist—yet; and possibly would never come to be, unless in some way, by giving all my mind to it, I forced it to become a reality. One thing was clear: we hadn't been really communicating sexually; she wasn't satisfying me, and obviously I wasn't giving her what she needed. Which, of course, was the crux of my new suspicion. But why couldn't I simply be honest with her, tell her, ask her to leave? I *had* asked her to leave, one morning not long after we arrived; but when tears came to her eyes tears also came to mine and I begged her to forgive me, and to never leave. So, now I'd been reduced to the insanity of following her; and it had me feeling crazy with rage and shame and self-hatred. Yet, I could not turn back.

> She continued to follow the ocean and I continued to follow her. And I wasn't worried about her suddenly turning around, seeing me. She never looked back and even when she looked to the side, she never saw *people,* not their *faces.* She never really *focused* on anybody who wasn't directly in front of her. When Oni walked on the street she was so consumed by her own emotion and her own motion that the world around was merely fused, like an audience. And she was that way long before she became a professional actress.

Earlier, at the beach, we'd had an argument about the presidential election going on in the United States. It was meaningless and silly. No, it wasn't meaningless but it was still silly and I have the feeling that we both were even then aware that we didn't give a shit about the election and that who the next president would be really wasn't what was bugging us.

> I followed her on across Rodriguez, the street on which we lived in a vast Spanish-style apartment with a great balcony running on two sides, one side facing the beautiful blue ocean,

the *bahia,* and the other, the purple and green mountains. Oni moved slower going past the makeshift fruit and vegetable and drygoods stands outskirting the large, cool, and enclosed marketplace where we often bought eggs. Once clear of the market area she climbed into a narrow, winding street, going toward the center of town.

Maybe she really was just out for a walk.

Suddenly she entered the red-and-white Dairy Queen ice-cream shop that catered to tourists. Like all the other business places here the front was wide open: no small square windows, no square oblong doorways. The sun seemed to be easing up as I took a seat in the park across from the shop, with my body, for the most part, hidden behind a thick low tree. But *I* could see her.

While she sipped her ice-cream soda I fought my shame and turned to the bay to watch the sun go down. It had now turned into a furious orange ball. And it was sinking very rapidly. Lovers stood on the malecon, watching now as they did every evening.

Briefly, I reflected on who I was, and where I'd come from and wondered at my being here. It was good, very good, despite everything.

At exactly seven-thirty the sun would sink, a blazing glowing round face, down into the ice-greenish-blue Pacific Ocean. You could set your watch by it. Many days I'd checked the electric clock the minute the sun fell into the ocean: and both were in correlation.

Lately, why'd I been shooting off the minute I entered her? Was there any truth to the theory of repressed hatred? If so, how much of it if any of it had to do with who we were socially? Worked up or not, where was the sense of mystery, of discovery? At a table near hers sat a pack of American college boys —white. They were eying her, elbowing each other and probably having a collective ejaculation. A middle-aged man, his wife and children, boy and girl, sat quietly—with too much stiffness and politeness, actually—on the other side of the sneaky, chattering, clowning boys. Now, I watched one boy get up, go over and bending slightly, resting his hand on the edge of Oni's table, say something to her. He was grinning and

174

wagging his head. Probably the American bit, you know: *Hi there!*

I watched Oni's face. She wasn't returning the smile. Well. I knew she'd had far more affairs with white boys than I'd had with white girls and I also knew, from her conversation, that the mystery, the excitement of a white boy, for her had long ago worn off: she, in fact, now found their sexual odor hardly more than dull to the senses; in fact, she spoke of past sex with white boys as though it, the memory, produced a sort of giddiness, like being sick from too much cough syrup. But with my natural suspicious mind I couldn't go without at least once giving in to doubt, the doubt that she possibly spoke this way for what she might have considered to be my best interest since most black men—while not fearing white men as sexual rivals—do resent the bloody history of the physical marriage of black women and white men, that began in the slave and slaveholder syndrome. Oni and I never had overt discussions about any of this, though on occasion our words touched the edges of this simple reality of American history. We both, after all, had come out of both a black and a white reference. The real question that faced us now was, in sexual and personal terms, how to get beneath the surface, the dense clichés of our common experience, to penetrate and understand and come away from the ultimate depth of those personal encounters.   Yes, I could be *this* "wise" even at such an insane moment as that moment in which I sat there spying on her and yet, not be able to pull myself away from these deadly games, to give up my destructive devices. After all, destruction was really what I wanted and was waiting to have.

> There she sat eating the ice cream she so often complained about. After a moment of the cold treatment from Oni the boy went back to his friends. Obviously he'd thought himself the bravest among them and now they each were red in the face from laughing at him. And he sat there blushing and playing with a straw.

What I felt was a stormy mixture of disappointment and relief. I began to wonder if I were on the verge of psychosis. *But I'm so logical, I can't be crazy!* Maybe I'm some sort of repressed homosexual—no, I know better than that; I've looked into these rigid categories very closely and I certainly know that the definitions themselves are fucked up. That homosexual bit is the everyday unreasoning worry of too many half-educated young men. It produces in them the same sort of tension that fear of cancer produces in middle-aged women. What I instinctively knew but intellectually had yet to make peace with was that I was neither homosexual nor heterosexual nor any other kind of *sexual*. I was simply my sexual self. And if I couldn't satisfy Oni I should have the guts to find somebody I could satisfy. It was that simple.

> At the end of no matter what I say I'll feel that there's a deeper unturned layer of truth. Anything and nothing can be proven. It's that loose.

Oni sat there as though listening to her stomach, waiting for its message, its thanksgiving or complaint. She left a few pesos on the table, got up, and went toward the sidewalk. A blond young man I'd seen somewhere before stopped her at the point where the sidewalk began. They exchanged greetings. She even gave him a half-hearted smile. Now, he was talking, with his arms folded across his chest, and she was listening. He was wearing dark glasses and an opened peon-style white shirt and light-blue short pants. As he talked his big hairy sunburned arms were folded across his chest. As Oni listened to him she shifted the weight of her body from one leg to the other. And she was focused directly on his face as his mouth continued to open and close.

> Oni stepped around the young man rather abruptly but he followed her across the hot bumpy street to the elevated surface of the plaza where I was sitting in the shade of a tree. She still hadn't seen me when she sat on a bench facing the bay, near the taxi-cab stand. The young man followed her and sat beside her, crossed his legs and leaned forward to look directly into her face as he spoke. She shook her head. Negative. From across the plaza her naked knees and legs looked very appealing. I was almost hypnotized, watching the swinging motion of her suspended foot. The sandal flapping against the bottom of it. Her arms crossed, looking away from the man as he rapped.

My point wasn't yet proven. I fought a happy misery. But fight is not always struggle.

BLACK MAN SLAYS 4
& SELF

Caption from a clipping. I was looking in one of Oni's drawers for her speed pills. She was still asleep at eleven thirty in the morning and I'd had a shower and still felt like shit so, maybe a little amphetamine would do the trick. I didn't find the synthetic amines there but folded neatly and tucked between two pairs of pink panties I found that Oni had placed three different clippings from newspapers. The subject of each was the same: Moses Westby's killing of four people and himself. They were each more or less the same.

So she *knew* and she'd never mentioned it.

For her, our apartment was too comfortable. Why did we, like white folks, have to live in this luxury?

I gave in.

Oni wanted a more primitive way of life and in search of it (though, without giving up our apartment) we paid $8 each (along with a group of about twenty other foreign suckers) for a roundtrip ticket for what was billed as a pleasure cruise to a village about three hours away. It was said to be an Indian village situated at the foot of a mountain and facing the ocean. Not many tourists there, and we could easily find a hut somewhere in the mountains. We had simply to first locate an old Indian who owned several of the houses and could rent us one. Going along on the pleasure cruise was cheaper than renting a boat and hiring some one to sail us there.

The trip was disastrous, to say the least.

I think what I resented from the very outset was that Oni had the attitude that we, too, were on a pleasure cruise, and her obvious excitement over it and how that whole frame of mind she displayed contradicted this business about wanting a more primitive way of life. I mean, if you want to live in a mud hut and rough it you aren't supposed to get worked up over a fucking pleasure cruise. I saw it simply as a painful necessity to get to our point. But she'd dressed up like she was going to a damn party.

And you know already that the distance from one side of a "puddle" to the other is not far enough: since the trip creates pressure, pressure becomes a problem.

Oni wore a violently red mini dress, some sort of transparent panties, and her sandals. She captured everybody's eyes. On the way over the guide pointed out the jutting area of land where a Hollywood company had recently shot a movie.

Legally nobody except Indians in the area could actually own property in the tiny village. We searched the hills but couldn't find the old Indian landowner; however, a young American white man who'd been swimming in the river (a low river, we walked across) directed us to the only house at the moment that was for rent. In his wet swimming trunks, trying to be excessively friendly but obviously self-conscious and nervous, he led us up a narrow path to the place. The American explained that, if we liked the house, we could stay overnight at the Lagunita Hotel and tomorrow morning when the owner returned we could settle the deal with him. Well, we'd see.

I didn't like the house. And the young man stood outside, embarrassed, while we argued. (Later, she was *glad* that I had been so emphatically against it: *she* wouldn't have stood up very long under the pressure of buzzing bugs and no electricity no hot water and no edible food. Besides, that nice young man had other American friends living in those hills and *I* certainly didn't leave the United States to come live among an encampment of its citizens.)   Anyway, going back, she wouldn't walk beside me. She lagged behind, with the nice young man. And, when, at one point I tried to take her arm just before descending a steep drop in the path, she pulled away so energetically, so quickly, she lost her balance and fell, skinning her knees. And she refused to let me help her up; of course, the young man saw *everything* as she lay there deliberately (I think) exposing herself. Those transparent panties. Probably still embarrassed, the white boy walked a few steps beyond us, waiting, and looking down the mountainside, toward the ocean.

Oni finally got up and immediately ran ahead, and began walking alongside the guide, though the path really wasn't wide enough to accommodate two abreast.

About halfway down the young American stopped and said, I guess you folks can make it from here; just continue to follow the path. I live in that house over there.

Oni gave him a frozen smile then walked on. The path was still very difficult and steep. Branches hung into it and had to be moved or they'd hit you.

At one point she stopped   turned, and waved at the young man climbing the path to his house.

When I caught up with her and tried to reason with her she simply rolled her pretty eyes furiously, looking at me.

At another point she stuck her fingers in her ears and started humming while I was gently teasing her for being so childish.

Then, quite suddenly on a rock beside the path she sat down, holding her knees propped so that her elbows bedded against them comfortably, her fists supporting her angry, lovely face.

You make me sick. Why'd you just go ahead and leave me alone?

But Oni—I started.

Listen, she said, go to the bar down there and get drunk or something . . .

I stood there silent and brooding feeling helpless, trying to control my growing anger.

From where I stood, down below I clearly saw the shimmering blue river water with its white-skinned swimmers and the yellow-white sand and the thatched roof hotel and a few huts beyond, dotting the beach. The river wiggled out into the ocean where the sun was at full blast. And we had two or three hours yet before the boat was due to return us. I looked at Oni. The path was very steep and I was reluctant to leave her but she was very pissed. And when she was like that she was best left alone.

So. I continued the slow climb down and at the river took off my shoes again and waded across. On the other side now I passed near an old drunk Indian lying on the hot sand and murmuring to himself. As I went by he gave a halfass wave. Standing in a small patch of grass near the mouth of the river were three fat grazing cows. Rare creatures in this part of the world.

I found a seat, a beach chair near the bar and restaurant of the hotel. The tourists, sipping their cool drinks, occasionally looked at me out of the sides of their eyes.

180

I thought of going back but I only sat there watching the ocean. An hour passed and she still hadn't come down from the mountain. My stomach began to churn. I was sweating and I felt very sick. I could hardly breathe.

What I felt was something like terror.

I couldn't sit still any longer. I started off across the sand, but not in the direction of the mountain where I'd left Oni. The beach ended and I began to climb into a wooded area behind the huts where naked Indian children were playing in mud pools with thick hogs and small, skinny pigs. A single chicken was strolling around, cackling and bobbing its head.

I stopped and stood for a moment in the shade of a tree, smelling my own sweat and listening to the wild beat of my heart. Behind me, the sounds of the ocean, and near me, the gentle rustle of leaves and the grunting of the hogs and pigs and the laughter and language of the children. Then suddenly, *churp churp churp   churp   churp   churp* sang a bird.

We started piling onto the boat. Oni still hadn't come back. The idea of leaving her somehow appealed to me for a moment then I felt ashamed of the thought and began worrying. I'd better go look for her. I asked the guide in Spanish to wait for me, then started out across the sand toward the river and the mountain. Halfway across the sand, I saw her running toward me. On her toes she was running across the river and the water splashing all around her.

Halfway back the sky began to cloud and the sun went in hiding. Oni sat beside me but we didn't speak during the entire trip back.

By the time we were out of the boat, on the malecon, walking toward our apartment building, we were under the full blast of the usual evening shower. This was the beginning of the rainy season. And the rain felt good. A pretty white girl, about eighteen, coming toward us, looking directly at me, made her eyes do something very flirtatious. Oni, too, saw it.

The little bitch!

Why, Oni, does she have to be a little bitch?

But to my question there was no answer.

181

I lay on one of the twin beds looking at the ceiling. Oni was taking a shower and when she came out she sat on the side of the other bed, drying her hair.

I guess I may as well tell you, you probably suspect it anyway —me and the white boy fucked, she said.

I said nothing.

She continued. First, we did it against a tree, so we could watch the path, in case you came back. Then, it got good, and we didn't care anymore; so we stretched out on the ground. But you don't have to feel bad, Moses; he wasn't any good. I could've done better with my *own* little finger.

The terror I'd felt had now exploded and what was left in me was something very quiet. I felt empty, I felt sad.

Suddenly she came over and sat beside me. Placed her hand on my thigh. I'd stripped and was lying there naked.

Are you mad at me?

No, Oni.

Suddenly she laughed.

Ants got all over my back, she said. All over my neck and even up my ass. Those fucking ants really move fast. And gnats! WHEW! I always thought it'd be romantic to fuck out under the open sky, but *boy!*

Silence.

I'm bad for you, aren't I?

Maybe we're bad for *each* other, I said.

Yeah.

Silence.

Do you want to separate?

I didn't because I couldn't answer her—yet.

Tell me it's all a bad, bad dream. But I won't believe you.

> A kind of safety valve: I tell myself, Leave Oni; otherwise,
> you're going to end up insane, at the bottom of your own most
> terrible nightmare.

We've been here six weeks and now we're about to move on.
To try to find another "pretty" place.

> I don't want to be just *on* a male ego trip yet I can't escape
> the fact that she's damaged some part of me that cannot be
> photographed, some very elusive segment that I trusted her to
> protect. What *I've done to her* is another question. And not
> unequal to my own.

We're packed, waiting for the taxi that the travel agency promised
to send between nine and nine-fifteen. Oni got up early this
morning and cleaned the apartment. It was the first time she
ever bothered. Two weeks ago we stopped the maid and all of
her thieving children from coming to water the plants, sweep
the floors, bring clean towels and sheets, because my underwear,
large quantities of dexedrine, darvons, Miltown, nembutol, dexa-
myl spansule, even Oni's birth-control pills, everything, to say
nothing of loose change lying around or in my pockets—anything at all, rapidly vanished when they came around. The
owner of the building, Señor Reinoldo Rubin, a tall heavy
light-skinned man who spoke perfect English, had initially
recommended the maid. When he heard of the dismissal he came
to our opened doorway and in his typical pleasant manner asked
what had gone wrong. Rather than tell him that the maid he
sent was a fluttering and bootlapping and grinning thief I
simply said that we couldn't afford her services. The expression

on his face said he didn't believe me. About a week after we'd stopped the maid, when I was no longer angry, I realized that *she and her children had to steal*. And though Oni and I weren't rich and could never convince them of this fact and though we ourselves came from a slave class the other stigma, being Americans, that alone gave them the right to *take us* whenever they could. So, I felt guilty for having let her go and yet I could not keep her because I could not *knowingly* let her steal what we had—and we had *so* little.

We're waiting for the taxi. I'm sitting at the white table, which is just inside the large main room, close to the balcony that looks toward the bright ocean and, the clear high blue unending sky. Sometimes two showers or thundershowers come every evening now. But the dampness and the mist are brief and soon again the sun shines. However, at the moment everything is gray except a dirty red truck and it is morning. From where I'm sitting I can see and hear a heavy, overloaded bus coming up the road and on top of it along with huge boxes and shabby suitcase are crates of excited chickens. Every morning at this time it pulls out of this town, loaded with poor people, and travels about two hundred miles to another town, making many stops along the way. In the evening, there's another one that does the same thing.   A peon beneath a large sombrero drives a pack of burros slowly this way, coming up from *Arroyo de Cuale* (but it is not a dry creek bed) and sometimes called *Rio de los Muertos*—river belonging to the dead. Even from here, looking to the side, I can see the women down there pounding their clothes against the rocks, stripped down to half-slips and bras. The old people, I often wonder about their pain. How they *live* with it without the relief of drugs. And they actually spend their lives in those little huts that are never shown on the picture postcards.

I feel very sad, I feel very frustrated.

The *burrero* (or asskeeper), with his animals, now pass beneath the balcony. I can only hear them, their small hoofs on the packed bed of rocks, purple, blue gold yellow green red.

What's the matter with me? I feel on the verge of tears!

I realize I'm going to miss all of this. The man who rents horses is coming up the road from the river. Near a spot where

184

buzzards are feeding on something dead, also near the river, beautiful children squat in the grass playing quietly.

This afternoon, after the glow of the sun, after the usual brief rain, it will be impossible, for a moment, to look directly at the ocean. The sun will be dropping rapidly and the horizon of the ocean will be sharp, blindingly distinct, a vanishing point no eye can focus on. And maybe a herd of bulls will be driven up Hidalgo from the river, maybe one will be upset by a coming truck and almost stampede the entire herd, nearly trampling a tiny beige VW automobile. It happens frequently.

Blazing white suds were whipping at the ends of the murky clay-colored inner tides, and the ocean was the same blue the sky held and you could hardly see where one ended and the other began.

Oni and I hardly talk anymore. Walls. Walls between us. Why're we leaving and where're we going?

We're somewhere else. It is highland, cool, dry. And the sunlight, it is thin.

We were out walking and stopped in front of a church near the marketplace. I was casual but Oni was wearing a mint-colored jersey of fluid rayon and standing against the pink flesh-colored brick fence surrounding the paved frontyard of the grand *Templo del Oratorio de San Felipe Neri;* she looked astonishing! I almost liked her again.

> In New York people piss shit eat die do anything on the street and I wasn't surprised to see a white man, or any man, wetting against the church wall in this very religious village. Judging from the way he was dressed he was an American. And he was very drunk. But the natives here have long complained that visitors do not respect their customs.   The pisser is a chubby, well-dressed middle-aged man. If he were a native already the local cops would be hauling him away to jail where he'd have to, as punishment, ring the church bells all night and into the morning.

Playfully a little girl crawls right up to the wall and begins to ferociously sniff the jagged oval wet spot. She's a dog, she's funny. But the pissy drunk man hasn't noticed her; and he stumbles off down the path through the market place. If his swagger suggests his origin, he's from Texas. He goes forth, his peter juggling before him; while the natives all around begin to giggle and snicker.

> The look on Oni's face is one of disgust.

That's why I don't like my father, she said.

What'd you mean?

Liquor! She spoke the word as though it were nasty tasting.

Those were the first words exchanged between us in days. I caught myself. I still felt resentful. And I stood there watching the little girl on her knees. She was sniffing around the wall and the ground where the piss was steaming and I wondered if one day the urine test would move beyond hospital walls toward a larger research effort. Dogs, for example, are not entirely without smarts and they find it a most valid method of discovering specific identities.

My eyes are always getting hung on things. But only on the things that are important. As we continued through the bumpy market place, stepping around the ropes stretched from the canvas tops of the stands to the pegs embedded in the ground, I got hung on the faces all around. Faces and hands, a dark hungry hustle reaching out, begging me to *buy*.

Poverty here, I saw, was different from poverty where I'd come from. There is a lean, lean possibility that even the poorest man in the United States may somehow manage one day to get a job and feed himself and his family. Here, such a possibility for most of the people seemed out of reach. The rich here were very rich and the poor, very poor. Nothing in the middle. Static.

In our new temporary home the ceiling was high. The walls were rough and whitewashed. Our apartment was in a large house on top of the highest hill, overlooking the small city. But there was no ocean and I missed it very much.

I built a fire in the fireplace early this morning. But the deep chill, even now at the warmest time of day—late afternoon, is a bit much. Yet Oni likes it here. For some reason I can't deal with she likes it better here than in that warm, seaside village we left. But from the moment two boys drove us in an old American station wagon from the airport, which was only a wide field of dense grass, since that time I've had a head cold. Bad. Shivering, I now get beneath the cool clean white sheets, feeling the heavy comfort of the blanket topped by a pale-green spread. And Oni is dressing to go to market . . .

It's almost like an obsession. I'm following her *again!* It's compulsive as hell, because I can't do anything about it though I want to turn back.

I'm on the other side, about two blocks behind her. Her eyes are suddenly caught by a boy of about seventeen who actually runs to catch up with her. They are side by side. He moves along with an angry hustler's stride, a kind of hip-grinding walk, tipping easily over the rocks; the rough but frosty eyes of old and young women digging *him and her* from cool, dark doorways.

I walk faster. Don't want to lose them.

He's talking to her and she's smiling, nodding her head. He's not a tourist, he's obviously a native.

She walks ahead of him. Goes across the bridge but looks back to see if he's following—and he is. She smiles. Her strides are brisk and the boy walks slowly, with his hands in his pockets. Eyes dead on her.

Oni goes along the river toward the old Medieval church abandoned on a small bluff.

I slow down, drop back, to stay out of sight.

The grass is thick near the church; quickly he climbs the bluff and circles a tree behind the church. Standing behind a bush on the side of the road I can see them both. She's looking up, as though awed by the old structure.

The shadows created by the limbs of trees here are massive. And it is a cool, gloomy spot. There're many tiny trees and bushes around the bigger ones and they all surround the old Christian ruins, spreading even thicker on the far side where the remains of a chapel is hardly visible. Nearby and overhead a few birds twitter in the excitement of fertility.

The boy stops circling the tree.

He goes and peeps into the church through a small, round window in the side. His head moves like a bird's.

I look at Oni. My heart is pounding. She's very lovely. She's wearing a bright above-the-knee dress of about three layers of gauzy bluish white shimmering material with an apple-shaped sequined pattern. She's watching the boy and lingering in that subjective, delicious smile of hers.

The old church. *Phew!* What a huge and noble and pretentious edifice! Yes, even at this moment—no, *especially* at this moment—I can be captured by such a giant relic of vanity! a thing from a dwindling age and spirit of moral authority, of a dark Medieval entrenchment of the heart, still lurking and whispering here beneath these trees, with no charisma left, it seems to have become its own grandest heresy! And the thought flashes through my mind that though Thursday and her church folk, all those people who forced Oni and I to marry just for *their* merriment, never had a house of worship quite as grand as this, their material poverty, nevertheless, was never as tragic as that of the millions of worshipers who've passed through these doors, giving not only coins they couldn't afford to give but also giving their total lives to a mystery none of them can ever penetrate.

> The boy *knows* she's watching him; he pulls away from the window and walking disappears at the rear of the church. Abruptly. Like he'd seen something inside and was seeking a way in.

Oni climbs the steep and sudden path close to the wall and stops at the window where the boy had stood. She now looks in. Her back slightly bent, to adjust her head more precisely to the level of the opening.

> She, too, now follows the path to the rear.

I follow. I watch myself putting one foot in front of the other. I like my sandals but one of the straps is about to break. And the steps up to the door of the old church are uneven and anybody could easily fall trying to ascend them. For a moment I'm so swept away by *the vanity* of that huge bolted doorway my head rattles.   The bricks, everywhere, are cracked. Vines climbing the walls. Lizards hanging on the ancient woodwork. A busy colony of ants moving into a crevice of the brick step where I stand. I continue up this way to get a closer look at the elaborate giant doorway. The *tallness* of men in their own minds.

> I could see nothing through the little window but I heard the wings of birds beating with their frightful cry.

I continued to the back and, sunk slightly below the surface of the ground, caked with mud, standing ajar, a door. The space was large enough for entrance.

It opens into a distorted oblong cool darkness.

I still hear the birds, but nothing else.

My stomach growls. My eyelids are jumpy. The birds stop.

But I have now a whiff of Oni's perfume. I continue, slowly.

Now, I hear the soft echoes of speech but the words are not clear. And the birds start again.

I go on. Obviously I'm walking along a long hallway toward the main area of the house of worship. The place is stifling, so airless. I can hardly breathe. I come to the end of the hallway and see a wide space of busted benches and piles of junk against either wall; and there are old, broken stained-glass windows stretching all the way up to the ceiling and in the ceiling itself but the artwork is cheap, very terrible.

I push spider webs out of the way and continue. Their voices are becoming clearer and the echoes are riding higher, among the trapped birds that have forgotten how they got in.

Now.

I see them. Oni and the boy. On the rotanda, before the altar. Side by side, on their knees, heads bent, palms of their hands clasped together as if in prayer.

And suddenly it is so quiet all I can hear is the huge struggle of my own breathing. As I watch them, their lips moving, in dead silence.

Even the birds have found a way out.

But for me, too often, it is like being still trapped inside an airtight, artificial nightmare.

I go to sleep and wake up.

Sleep wake up

early in a hypnopompic and frosty morning in a ghost town western scene straight out of Wyatt Earp and Doc Holiday, I'm looking from my bedroom window in the first house I remember. Veronica, Moses, are asleep in their bedroom.

Somewhere on some anxiety-ridden level of my mind I ask, *Where is Oni?* Did I leave her yet? Has she left me ?

I go into the room where Moses and Veronica are asleep and from the window the scene is the same.

What originally compelled me to look out the window? Yeah, now I remember. I'd heard the squeaking of the pulley: it sounded like the rusty wheel of a wheelbarrow and if you're in a very small town in one of the states that holds to the traditional myths of American "glory," where they grudgingly accept technology, hate the west and east coasts, call themselves men of justice who're pure in heart, wear overalls and carry lunch buckets, think of themselves as pioneers and superior beings because of the color of their skin, then you know how it is, how little old men push around wheelbarrows on the roads and streets before daylight opens the eyelids. Why they do this nobody knows. Well. I thought the squeaking was something like that and that the quaint figure would be interesting to steal a glance at. But it wasn't that sort of simple, acceptable imposition on the morning—I'd expected a view more up to date, one. And two, a uniformed Negro cop in a Tombstone City setting was at that hour a bit much. The colored cop was slowly pulling down a rope that was piling in a tangle at his foot. I looked up to see what the rope was suspended from and, there's a man, perhaps dead, and his body has been wrapped horizontally no less than a hundred times with the rope. His arms flat to his sides. He looks as stiff as a log. I can't make out whether he's black or white, brown or yellow. He's wearing gray-blue flimsy pants and I can see the bottoms of his shoes. In point of fact I think he's dead and the squeaky sound, it's clear, comes from the pulley over which the rope the cop is pulling on is suspended. The other end is around the ascending man's neck.

He is going up, slowly . . .

in jerks, caused by the resting periods the executioner allows himself. Standing near the cop are about a dozen old-time palefaces, mostly women in bonnets, all, except one, are looking *up*. The one who isn't looking up is looking straight at me, as I stand at the window. Also, I notice she isn't white. She has her

191

hair in a huge Afro, she's copper color and even from here I can see she has freckles. But like the others, who stand as still, as silent as snapshots in an old scrapbook, she seems strangely remote.

The only sound moving across the cool morning is the irregular creaking of the wheel, as the rope turns over it. One of man's most revolutionary inventions, this wheel.

But the cop continues to pull on the rope and the victim never reaches the top. Anyway, consider this: what possibly could happen *up there* to improve his death that couldn't happen on the way up?

I have the trustworthy feeling that Oni and I are definitely on the way down, over, and out! Which, of course, implies that we were at one time in my opinion *up* from somewhere. Up from slavery?

You never knew my dog, Ploddy, did you, Moses?

I used to see him.

Her.

All right, her.

Hmmmmm.

We were sitting on our balcony in the early evening watching the sun go down behind the mountains of this small religious city.

Actually, though, I said to Oni, I never knew anything about your life before or after we were married. So many things about you I don't know. Like, who you gave your cherry to. Your first love, things like that. So many things.

Her laugh was sudden and wild. Oni kicked her feet up, threw her head back, clapped her hands together, and screamed. Her face turned light purple as she turned to me with wet eyes.

Jesus, I never knew you were *interested. . . !*

Well, I said in low key, there *was* a time when I was interested.

But not now?

I thought it out. Yes, I was *still* interested, but only clinically. Or who was I kidding? Nevertheless, I said nothing for the

193

moment. I had the terrible feeling that if I were not careful I could bury myself beneath spoken words and lose touch with myself and the particular areas of reality I had so far been lucky enough to stumble on.

> You weren't always in Chickamauga, Moses; certainly not in the beginning. In any case, I don't remember you being there.

Oni suddenly giggled.

> I hardly remember myself. And then, even when you and that little creepy fat child, whatshername . . . Gal, when Veronica brought you two there, and left you, you were on a farm on Highway 69, while the rest of us black folk were living in Remus Road. So, you know, you people were on the other side of Sodacracker Heights, between the graveyard and the woods. We always sort of envied you all, because it seemed you had so much more than we had. You had a piano and flowers in the front yard. You had apple trees, fig trees, grape vines, hogs and chickens, and mostly we had to work for the white folks.

Thursday, I said, was washing and ironing for them.

> Yeah, I know, but not every day, she didn't have to break her back like my people did. Anyway, I just mentioned that not to get hung up on it but just now for the first time it comes consciously to my mind that we, the people in Remus Road, were jealous of the Flower people. I remember well that feeling. But also thought you all were pretty fucking strange, man, did you know that?

I think, somewhere, deep down, I knew it.

> Yeah, said Oni.

Then, we sat there, each silent; and coming up the narrow sidewalk below, I could hear the old peon shouting, selling the only English-language newspaper available. The shouting ended and the newspaper-seller started imitating a donkey. He had a truly cynical sense of humor, but his load was heavy and I wondered what passed through his mind when he saw tourists, like us, taking it easy and buying whatever we wanted as though money came so easily we never had to even think of it. Certainly he had a right to be cynical and to imitate a donkey if he wished. It was enough to damage a man's sex life, to say the least.

However, the silence between Oni and me had now gone on so long I felt an overwhelming need to hear her if not both of us talk. *Talk talk, please talk to me Oni talk.*

Do you remember Mr Herman McHerring? she asked.

No.

I didn't think you would. He was a janitor at school but I think you'd moved back to the city when this happened. Anyway, he was the first. A white man.   A long pause. She cleared her throat   . He was always after us kids, especially us first-graders and it was holy hell if any of us were caught inside the building during recess or lunch time, so when I sneaked through the building (a short cut to the playground) I was always quiet and reeeeeeal fast, like ZOOM, Road Runner! But this one time he saw me and came running after me.

She paused. Dreamy. Lost in her reflections.

. . . His big hands scoop me up into his arms and I'm kicking him, still giggling cause he runs so funny and I try to bite him, too; and he's holding me tight, saying, "Didn't I tell you kids not to come in the building during lunch time?" And I'm not really even scared of him but he smells nasty like a big grumpy waterbuffalo and I plead, you know, just play-beg him with sugar-coated words like, Oh please pretty sweety honey pie please sweet please oh sweet please let me go please let me let me O Mister Big Bad Wolf let me go! And he has me against his chest, facing him, and I'm talking in his face, and we're all alone down in that dreary basement. Do you remember that basement? No? Anyway, I feel his hands moving between my legs and he's holding me and beginning to smile so I like him because I know he won't really be bad or mean to me and he's just teasing me and will soon let me go. I really thought that. I really did. But the main thing is I don't want him to tell my old mean teacher Mrs. Poyser who I don't like cause she smells like shit and she shouts at me when I chew gum or talk to my friends and she has a tight little mouth and she spanks us even when we haven't done anything.   Now Mr McHerring was going GRRRRRRRRRRRRRR GRRRRRRRRRRRRRR like he's a mad animal with vicious teeth ready to eat me yum yum

yum yum. And he says, "I'm gonna put salt and pepper on you, and gobble you for supper, if you don't stay outta this building during recess and lunchtime." Then one of my shoes dropped then I felt suddenly with my big toe that tail between his legs. I still remember how it felt.   Oni stopped. Lit a cigarette. She smoked for awhile before she spoke again. Then
Yeah. All men and little boys have them, too. I saw uncle Bob sticking his in mama making her grunt. That night when they thought I was asleep. Now I feel it some more and wiggle my toe against it cause I'm curious. I want to see it up close, but I don't know how to ask him to let me see it. I know they swell up big when you play with them. I saw my brother's. I saw him in the bathroom washing it one day. I peeped through the key-hole. I know he sticks it in a lot of women and even in horses. That's what everybody says. So Mr. McHerring's is getting big cause he's a big man and his arms make me feel funny all over like I felt that time looking through the keyhole at Eric's.

I stopped her. I said, You sound as though you're *re*living it.

Yeah yeah. Where was I?

Wiggling your toe against—

Oh yes! Wiggling my toe against it he begins to lick my neck with his *phew!* tobacco-smelly tongue. So I go *Yek yek!*

Yek yek?

Yes! *Just* listen, Moses! So I told 'em I knew what that thing was down there and he wanted to know *how* I knew so I told him I'd seen my uncle's and my brother's. Meanwhile, he's still walking with me in his arms. *Not* taking me outside, mind you! So he starts licking my ear like he's some sort of dog, y'know. And he asks me, "Say little girl, you ever fuck?" and I tell him, No, but uncle was going like this—and I start bumping back and forth against him and giggling. I was really silly then . . .

So what happened?

Huh? Oh, yeah . . .

With her sandal Oni mashed out her cigarette on the brick floor.

So he starts this business about how good it makes you feel to actually do it yourself. Much better than watching. Meanwhile he takes me into this dark furnace room and locks the door behind us. And I'm telling him that little kids like me don't suppose to do it, especially with grown people. You see, I'm getting scared by now. And he's still trying to convince me that everything's gonna be all right. That it won't hurt or nothing. And I should never tell my mama nor my father because they wouldn't *understand* . . .

Oni stopped again. This time, a longer pause.

I still . . . couldn't see . . . anything. It was . . . very, very dark. It was very   hot also   in there. But I really wasn't all that scared. I remember being disappointed because it was so dark and I couldn't see *it*. He put my hand on it but I still couldn't see the thing. It felt spongy like a turkey neck. He had me sitting on his lap facing him, with my legs around his waist. And . . . he . . . pulled my panties to the side . . . and started tickling me with it.

I looked at her. She suddenly seemed frightened and angry at once. I waited.

You know, she said, I think I'd *kill* any man who would ever do that to a child of mine!

After Oni opened up she went on for days. The subject depended on her mood.

> After breakfast, over coffee, dragging on cigarettes, we watched one another's eyes. But most of the sound came from her face.

You know, when I was sixteen I left Chickamauga; I stayed with my oldest sister, in the city.

> How'd you know you were sixteen?

I figured it out. Plus, I was stealing things from department stores. And that's the age, isn't it . . .

> Was it fun?

Didn't you ever steal anything, Moses?

> Sure; and when I was caught and they wanted to know my name I said I AM THAT I AM, and they wanted to know what that meant and I said, just say that I AM told you.

She laughed a little. Then, we were quiet.

> Things used to glitter, Oni said, and really attract me. When I was attracted to something . . . it was hard to keep my hands off.

I bet you were never caught.

> *Oh yes!* she said. Yes, I was caught—*once!*

You're kidding.

> No. It was during my first year in the city. In the beginning I wasn't very skilled but I got better. I learned my mistakes. You see, Oni said, there were these signs everywhere encouraging me, like NO OBLIGATION TO BUY. And everything, all this

stuff shimmering and glowing. And it'd become so easy to pick up small items, especially costume jewelry, that I'd gotten sort of careless. But I loved department stores! It wasn't so much the Sweet Sixteen shit that turned me on—what I wanted was to get my hands on a *real* diamond! While I was stealing something I always felt a good secret twitch in my cunt. I don't know if you can begin to imagine that! But the time I got caught I'd picked up this *unbelievably* expensive little bottle of Alexandra de Markoff's Countess Isserlyn Make-Up. And right over the counter there was this sign, I'll never forget it: BEWARE SHOPLIFTERS WILL BE PROSE-CUTED TO THE FULLEST EXTENT OF THE LAW. Anyway, I made it outside and really thought I was safe when I felt a hand softly touch my shoulder. I thought it was just some guy flirting, y'know.

Oni and I laughed together.

She continued. But I took a good look at him and he *wasn't* grinning and *that* scared me. A dauntless floor dick? Oh nuts! not now! I'm not ready! But he tugs. He takes me back inside with this pink plastic smile smashed all over his face. He was really delighted with himself, having caught me. But I kept shouting at him like I was innocent. I was really scared, man! My oldest sister could be a mean bitch and already I had weird visions of her having me placed in a reform school for girls. Y'know, a deeper prison . . . So I was saying, TAKE YOUR HANDS OFF ME! and he was pulling me by my arm and saying, "Just come along quietly, don't make things worse than they are . . ." and I'm saying, SHIT, YOU'RE HURTING MY ARM MISTER—LET ME GO! and he says, "I see, you want the handcuffs . . ." I knew who he was but I started pretending I didn't. Man, I was really performing! I said, Who ARE you? YOU'RE KIDNAPING ME—YOU HAVE NO RIGHT! But he pulled me into the vestibule and threatened to put the handcuffs on if I didn't cut it out. So I finally accepted the fact that I'd been caught and we went upstairs in one of those bright massive soundproof elevators and cross this endless carpeted floor and into this little office. There was this guy and this chick there, just waiting like they'd been expecting me or something. There were all these telephones on the desk, colors like pink green yellow red, and catalogs, and on the wall, a picture of the president of the store. I'd never before seen such a fancy office in all my life! So the three of them just stood there looking at me, not saying anything. And at that moment naturally I had a desire to be anywhere else, even stranded somewhere struck with amnesia in the middle of a November plaza of a seagull-infested village chilled by the damp odor of saltwater. Or even to be that town's central plaza's heroic statue stained by centuries of natural birdshit. And these psychic escapades were not simply the graphics of a dreamy and trapped girl's airy mind. No.

I never knew you could be *so* poetic, I said.

Oni laughed. I was *imitating* you.

Funny how people who live together begin imitating each other.

Yes, but it's not funny.

I still don't know for sure *why* I did it nor even if I meant to go so far; but it certainly brought a kind of end to everything.

I refer to the incident (actually, it was more than an incident) of jumping over the fence into that bullring in the midst of a bullfight.

I fell but scampered back to my feet and bustled across the ring toward this vicious bull even the *matador* was obviously scared of. I stood there, halfway in the sunlight, halfway in the shade where an oval line (reflected from the very top of the Plaza de Toros *oriente*) sliced the ground into two parts, one warm, one cool.

I felt foolish, of course, but I also felt very handsome and braver than I'd ever before dared feel.

Of course, the spectators all jumped up, very alarmed and there was a lot of calling and shouting in both Spanish and English but I paid attention to none of it, except, several times I glanced toward Oni, trying, but not too sternly, to make out her reaction. Yet, I wasn't doing it *for* her. I'm sure I would have done it, at that point in my life, or something like it, had she not been there at all.

I started immediately calling the bull; but right away, the *picador* on his horse, Don Quixote in shock, moved between me, a clowning figure. and the animal, an uncompromisingly serious figure.

And two of the four *matadores,* the one who was already in the ring and the one who had bravely challenged and killed the awesome third bull, both handsome Spaniards, were instantly moving toward the toro in huge efforts to whip confusion through him. Barking at him: *Toro! Toro!* and *Ahhhh Toro! Ahhhh Toro!* So agile they were, so sharp-edged!

But now the bull took off toward one of the bullfighters yet he stayed clear and the animal passed and, turning quickly the huge thing went toward the *picador,* but only for a moment, then he came in my direction and, just at the moment when I was running toward him. A moment of eclipse-mystery; I'm sure, looking back on it, I wasn't *consciously* ready to die!

Toro! Toro! I was calling.

And suddenly for the click of a moment I *hoped* I was dreaming.

And the crowd was in an uncommon uproar.

Meanwhile, one of the young men on foot who drive the spear-tipped sticks (*banderillas*) into the animals' thick necks, the one Oni had said had a cute ass which she'd been watching since the first minutes of the first *novillada* at four o'clock, was trying to tackle me. A slippery prince with black eyes in the back of my head—he'd never succeed!

But he *did* and pulled me out of the path of the charging black bull. Probably saved my life; meanwhile, stunned, surrounded by screaming and shouting and laughter and whistling and catcalls, I felt sure I must be dreaming or going mad. That this wasn't real.

And it was apparently getting to be a bit much for the bloody toro! However, I was kicking the young *banderillero* on the leg and the boy turned me free, yelping, he caught his own leg, trapped it in his hands and on one wobbling leg went hop hop hop from the ring to the fortress-like safety of the old stained and beaten barricade behind which now many male egos of *la corrida de toros* had experienced crises and chaos.

But now two young toreros were closing in on him, while the fourth and final, the bravest matador of the evening, so lean and brisk, in dark blue with rich cold gold beneath the flat-topped black hat worn at a catty angle, the shock of his beauti-ful Latin face, long sideburns, was trying to occupy the creature.

But the bullfighter looked anxiously toward me as the struggle centered around him and everybody roared from sublimated fear as the bull shot straight for the fighter, passing so close that the matador's arm was scraped.

I insist I don't know what I thought or felt and nobody has the authority to be absolute about it.

The *picador* with his long spear was turning around, around and around on his sadly dumb nervous horse and he was trying to professionally keep the shielded eye of his padded animal away from the heavy blunt meaty instrument, the scapegoat of this grotesquely happy *gran festivalde!*

I do know this, though, I felt, there, for the first time, in that ring, for those few moments, that I was no longer a victim. I was my own person and I could actually decide whether or not I wanted to go on living—I could play with the question. But never mind all that!

As I say, swinging and kicking I got away, getting a mixture of cheers and boos, screams and yelps from the spectators. And the animal was moving slowly, hesitatingly toward me. Considerable adaptive value: in a controlled condition. Those dreary colorful *banderillas* hanging from the tough peak of his tortured hump, tired but still quite strong, the animal came to a bleeding, cautious pause. I could smell his blood and the earth's dust. And my own sweat.

Now, a new action begins! Heckling and jumping brightly and insanely near the toro one of the banderilleros got only a slow, unprejudiced glance from the exhausted animal.

Slimey yellow bubbles dripped from his opened, vegetative mouth. Blood, red as beet juice formed a little black pool in the dust directly under his belly. Without his initial force, he was digging his hoofs into the soft gravel, on your mark get set ready go.

And for the first moment in the moments I'd been out there, like an exhibitionist—which I'd never before ever been—I became aware of my own shame and logical cold fear, all traced somehow in the slime of violent pleasure. How could I for one moment open the full furnace of my roofed conscience and actually crave my own death? *while fearing it?* I mean, who, then would inherit my Social Security Number? Yet, there was a clearing inside, where a specified "game" was commonly slaughtered and not just for sport or food, but actually out of a need, an alert and, cunning need *for* evil (Eve, evening blood, spells; the powers of demons, creeps called men have invested us with). No matter how many airy souls roam through space, I could not close my opaque mind to the existential concept of my own semiprecious—now, very possible death.

I remembered Grady's death and the flies.

I was beneath a voice near the fence. In American words it said, THAT'S JUST DISGRACEFUL! HE'S DISGRACING HIS RACE!

So pathetic was the motivation behind the comment I almost laughed but everything for the moment had frozen—in me.

I was closer to the bull than anybody and we were all standing still.

I felt that, if I could touch the bull's head, and survive such a feat, life, from this perhaps unworthy moment, would be invested with essence. In other words I had to give meaning to it and it had to contain courage. And at the same time I argued with the shallowness of it. With myself—with being.

Nevertheless, I reached carefully toward the bull.

He was bleeding and sweating and half dead *but* I touched his head and in a strange and beautiful way that single act became for me a living symbol of my own human freedom. The others in the ring, they came halfway but the crowd, at this point boomed a sound that split the plaza's spirit.

Then.

All movements and all sounds in the ring and even my own slender sense of self, stopped.

It was a long moment.

There wasn't even the force of breathing. That space was filled by a vacuum. Yet, a swollen and quivering moment smeared with the presence of an impassable sort of pleasant pain: the tension of terror!

The tortured and bloody animal lowered his head. Even though I stood only a few inches from the weapon of the bull's head, in this moment I might have easily taken this *warning*. I certainly *saw* him.

But I was enjoying the pain of my glory in the dying afternoon sunlight. That *must* be what was happening. That's an intellectual, *not* an emotional deduction. I have no real idea what was going on in me.

While I was touching the bull's head, with my right hand, I suddenly waved my left toward Oni and the spectators.

Then.

The bull brought his lowered head up, suddenly! Funny, how all kinds of little unexpected details come back. Somehow, at this intense moment, my eyes strayed, even *while* I *knew* I was going to be hit—possibly killed! Which makes me wonder now about my own private sense of comedy. What I think of *just life itself*. What I really feel, deep down. And all the basic questions about pure *meaning itself* that suddenly springs from such speculation.

THAT MAN IS GOING TO BE KILLED!!!! shouted a woman.

When I woke up it was a full hour before I began to put the pieces of myself together again.

I left Oni there and flew back to the States. It took awhile though to get over my guilt feelings. But like I always survive difficulty I survived those feelings.

As the plane took off from the open area I peeped out at the men standing on the ground. Mechanics, I guess. Waving good-bye. They always do that in Latin countries—friendlier than they are in the United States. Nicer people. As they waved their clothes beat furiously from the wind from the propeller. And I wondered if they actually *felt* as happy as they looked.

A moment later, I was looking down at the small city drop back lower and through the few dense low clouds even the magestic churches lost their looming capacity to strike reverence in the psyche. And the sudden sight of the Plaza de Toros and the bullring itself with the afternoon's thin sunlight cutting across it sent a brisk shudder through me.

I was the only passenger and the two pilots were the light-complexioned type you see swarming the larger cities, down there. They are always more nurtured by the spirit of that fair god who conquered them, than by the mystic food offered from the darker side, the subdued side of their historical experience. How much longer would the world go on denying and disrespecting that darker side? Now, we were winging low over this *bought* country. A place where ancient Indians could risk death by the jimson-weed poisoning while inducing a trance caused by it spells, just to catch a whiff of the odor of some thief; but if that thief was the white ghost from that distant self-pontified Medieval country which even the mighty powers of Rome couldn't entirely conquer, then, obviously the trance they were in revealed absolutely nothing except it possibly opened the thighs of dark women in exaltation, in the deep quiver of overpowering respect for that certain rapture brought by the paleface whose large weapons were simply another form of magic. But we all respect magic and that was possibly *why* these flyers, deeply sunburned from the good life, were flying an airplane. And it was also why, at that moment, I was flying toward what I believed to be a new beginning.

New York, N.Y. 1969